CROSSING THE SAGAMORE

This is a work of fiction. Names, characters, businesses, places, events, locales, and incidents are either the products of the author's imagination or used in a fictitious manner. Any resemblance to actual persons, living or dead, or actual events is purely coincidental

Copyright © 2019 by Mike Bernard. All rights reserved. This book or any portion thereof may not be reproduced or used in any manner whatsoever without the express written permission of the publisher except for the use of brief quotations in a book review. Printed in the United States of America First Printing 2019

Dedicated to

BC High Class of '81

Forever friends.

And for

John Krusz and Joe Sebeika

Forever young.

A hand slides an 8-track cassette into the car stereo. Music blares from the speakers.

"As I walk through

this wicked world

searching for light in the darkness of insanity

I ask myself, is all hope lost

Is there only pain and hatred and misery?"

-Elvis Costello

DORCHESTER, MASSACHUSETTS 1981

Everything changed in 1981.

The disco '70's were officially over. Ronald Reagan replaced Jimmy Carter as President. MTV aired its first music video 'Video Killed the Radio Star' by The Buggles. And me and my best friends graduated from high school.

There were five of us. Me, Jimmy, Kevin, Steve (aka Beef) and Joe. Jimmy named us 'The Norsemen' because he loved history, especially all that Viking shit, and we were inseparable since fifth grade. We grew up in Dorchester, a working-class town, about a stone's throw south of Boston made up of white Irish families defined by Catholic parishes. It was a tough, close-knit neighborhood of triple-decker houses that stood shoulder-to-shoulder, so close you could almost share leftovers through your kitchen window.

Kevin was the oldest of our group by a few months and that made him the first to get his license. At seventeen he looked twenty-one, which helped in the whole 'fake ID to buy us beer' department. There was an aura of toughness and confidence that surrounded Kevin. He just always seemed older. Kevin would pick us up in his grandfather's enormous Bonneville, a powerful beast of a car with a V8-engine and plush light-blue crushed velour bench seats that sat three across. The interior was so big and so wide that if someone slammed the brakes, it seemed like you would free-fall for about two minutes before you hit the dashboard. The speedometer was calibrated all the way up to 140 miles per hour. (Do cars even go that fast?) One time, Kevin got the needle over 100 MPH, but Beef looked like he was literally going to explode from fear, so Kevin reluctantly eased off and slowed down.

Kevin would spin his Cape Cod key chain into the car ignition, exhaust would blow past the DISCO SUCKS bumper sticker, and he would cruise the streets, slaloming past cars double-parked all over Dorchester. We called the car The Love Boat, and you could fit seven people in there comfortably. Twelve uncomfortably if you put kids in the enormous trunk, which Kevin did when he'd sneak people into the Braintree Drive-In.

But we hardly ever had seven people in the Love Boat. We had five. Just us. The Norsemen. Well, six if you counted Kevin's girlfriend Katie.

We all knew Kevin really liked Katie because he let her play the Boz Scaggs *Silk Degrees* 8-track all summer long. Like, all. Summer. Long. Over and over. Every time she was in the Love Boat, Katie would blare 'Lowdown' or 'Lido Shuffle.'

'*Lido...Oh, oh, oh, oh!*'

And Kevin would cringe.

For the record, Kevin detested Boz Scaggs. 'This is the kind of music you'd hear standing in line at JC fuckin' Penny,' he so eloquently critiqued, then yank the tape out as soon as Katie was out of earshot. (Although Kevin did think the name Boz was cool. Certainly, better than Meatloaf...but more on that later).

What you need to understand is, Kevin had three rules.

1. My car.
2. My stereo.
3. My music.

Simple as that.

Nobody touched Kevin's tapes. Ever.

Katie was the only one I ever saw touch them or ever make a music selection.

When Katie wasn't snuggled beside him, Kevin kept the other love of his life close by. His Holy Grail. A brown vinyl case that held his beloved 8-track tapes all neatly arranged in alphabetical order. Aerosmith. Boston. The Doors. The Cars. Oops, I meant The Cars, *then* The Doors. God forbid the tapes were ever out of order. Kevin would immediately remedy that mistake. Today, we call it OCD. Back then we just called it 'being a pain in the ass.'

Beside me in the backseat sat Joe and Steve...I mean Beef. Joe gave him that nickname back in sixth grade. Not because he was 'husky' (a term used by fat kids' moms to help them feel less fat) but because his family ran the corner Deli and Beef always smelled like lunch meat and pickles.

Joe was the cool one of our group. He had long hair, a quick wit, and was always three steps ahead of the crowd. When everyone was watching Saturday Night Live, Joe was watching Monty Python's Flying Circus. When we thought we were cool listening to The Police, Joe was rocking out to English Punk bands we hadn't heard of yet like The Cure and Talking Heads. None of us had ever heard of Neil Young let alone Crosby, Stills and Nash. Joe made us play the 'Live Rust' tape on repeat that whole summer our Junior year.

'Oh, to live on Sugar Mountain, with the barkers and the colored balloons.'

The front seat of the Love Boat was reserved for the tapes, Katie, or Jimmy Callahan, and not necessarily in that order.

Kevin and Jimmy grew up on the same block, went to the same grammar school, same church, same middle school and same high school. Jimmy was thin and meek, one of those guys whose knee always bounced in the resting position. Jimmy always seemed nervous, and because he was so frail, he was a target for the bigger kids in the neighborhood. Jimmy realized early on that he needed someone to hold onto so he could survive. Luckily, he found Kevin. Once they saddled up together, no one was gonna fuck with Jimmy. I'm pretty sure Kevin was the main reason Jimmy didn't get swallowed up on the streets of Dorchester.

That is, until Old Man McShane came into his life.

Seamus McShane. We called him 'Old Man' McShane, but most of Dorchester knew him as 'that Irish prick'. Jimmy's mother remarried him after Mr. Callahan died a few years ago.

That's when everything started to go bad for Jimmy.

Real bad.

****

Like every Saturday, Kevin stopped the Bonneville at a house in disrepair. Faded St. Paddy's decorations hung alongside Christmas lights. It was June.

Old Man McShane sat on a worn couch on the front porch in his wife beater t-shirt, a Celtic cross tattoo on his forearm, drinking a mid-day beer and looking up and down the street like a sentry. Kevin beeped the horn just to piss him off.

Jimmy waved to us from his bedroom over the porch to let us know he'd be down in a minute. Then he slid a black guitar case from under the bed, threw it on the mattress and snapped the silver buckles open. It was empty, and Jimmy was pissed. He grabbed the case and ran out to the street.

"Where did you get that?!" Jimmy yelled at the two redheads playing with a baseball bat in the side yard.

We all hated Old Man McShane but detested his two redheaded sons Ronan and Corey even more.

Jimmy grabbed the bat from Ronan's hand.

"I'll take anything I like," Ronan, the older and crazier of the two, sneered. "Pussy American sport anyway."

Kevin leapt out of the car as if he were electrocuted. Nobody fucked with Jimmy as far as Kevin was concerned. Even though Kevin was bigger and could clearly kick his ass, Ronan stood his ground. He was that psycho.

The two of them squared off, about to throw hands, but Beef, always the peacemaker, stepped in between them with a plastic yellow wiffleball bat

"Here. Just use this," he said.

As he turned to leave, Ronan hauled off and whacked him across the back of the legs. Beef winced in pain. Kevin lunged at Ronan, and was hit by the other redhead, Corey. Punches were thrown wildly. Kevin had Ronan in a headlock, nailing him with punches to the head, while Jimmy and Corey rolled on the ground.

That's when Old Man McShane came down from the porch. It was almost as if he was enjoying the fight. That is, until one of his kids started losing. He cuffed Jimmy by the collar of his navy-blue Barracuda jacket.

"Those guys were in my room!" Jimmy yelled, red-faced angry.

McShane leaned in close to Jimmy, but we could all hear him.

"You listen here now," he snarled. "These two, they're me blood. Something you'll never be. If they want to use your shit, they'll use your shit. You hear me?"

Jimmy's mother came to the door attempting to help, but Old Man McShane looked up and sneered her into retreat, like he always did. Mrs. Callahan was forty but looked sixty. She had worn eyes and always wore a tired expression on her face that was clearly the result of a life lived in fear and sadness since her husband passed away.

McShane turned his attention back to Jimmy who was doing his best to hold back the anger and tears.

"I said, do you hear me boy?!" he growled, then hauled off and smacked Jimmy across the face.

"Yes," Jimmy replied, his shoulders slumped and his spirit broken.

"Yes, what?!" McShane spat, awaiting the answer.

"Yes, *sir*," Jimmy said, his voice so low it was nearly audible.

I remember a few things from that awkward moment. I remember wincing and looking away so Jimmy wouldn't be embarrassed. I remember the redheaded brothers, Corey and Ronan, smiling a sinister shitty little smile that showed their crooked yellow teeth. But what I remember most was how Kevin never took his eyes off Old Man McShane. His rage was boiling, ready to explode.

As we all climbed into the Love Boat, Kevin noticed a trickle of blood on Jimmy's lip. Without saying a word, he handed Jimmy a napkin from a bunch tucked underneath the car seat. It was an unspoken ritual they had done far too many times.

Kevin silently put the car in drive, and we peeled out for Cape Cod.

****

This was our routine and our escape.

Beef would hang out the window, raise his arms above his head and scream, "Rock and Roll!" and we'd hit the highway, letting Dorchester and the McShanes and everything else fade in the rearview mirror.

Driving over the Sagamore Bridge was like crossing over to another world. Joe would lift the Pioneer speaker covers from the back dash and reach into the cooler conveniently located in the trunk and hand out beers. Then we would blast the music. Loud. Like, really, *really* loud.

Within a year, the first Sony Walkman would hit stores causing a generation of kids to slap on earphones and listen to music alone. Not us. We enjoyed the unity of our music. There was power in it, a power that seemed to make us invincible. 'Made Loud to Play Loud' was the motto and we pumped our songs up as high as the volume would go.

I remember how Jimmy would smile wide as the car crossed the bridge, his head leaning out the window, his eyes closed as he felt the warm salt air on his face.

Six best friends riding south to the flexed arm of Cape Cod.

It was the time of our lives.

JFK made Hyannis the place to go in the 1960's and people, especially Irish Catholic people from Boston, flocked to grab small two-bedroom cottages on Cape Cod in the summer. We certainly weren't the Kennedys, something my mother would remind me of any time I wanted to buy something or broke something or left food on my plate.

'Who do you think we are, the Kennedy's?'

While the rich kids from Hingham and Cohasset went to areas like Chatham and Dennis, we found our escape on a sandy beach hidden in West Yarmouth on Lewis Bay, a small inlet off Hyannis Harbor where the calm waters look like a flat pane of ocean glass.

When Jimmy was young, Mr. Callahan used to rent a buddy's cottage on a hidden dirt road, and they would spend a week there every July. As soon as the family station wagon was unloaded, Mr. Callahan would walk the family down the sandy path straight to the beach. They would skip rocks along the water and walk along the bay at low tide looking for shells and periwinkles. The floors of the cottage would get all sandy and Jimmy would stay up way past his bedtime, but nobody minded because everyone was in such a good mood. Mr. and Mrs. Callahan would laugh and dance to old Mills Brothers and Ink Spots records played on an old Realistic turntable. They didn't even go to church that first Sunday of their vacation. (Although Mrs. Callahan made them double-up and go twice one weekend in September).

Those were some of the happiest times of Jimmy's life, and every chance he got to escape to this place trying to recapture it, we were happy to join along.

Once we made it to the beach at Lewis Bay, we'd march down to the shore and lean against an old overturned Dory rowboat. The seagulls and gentle surf gave a stark contrast to our noisy, gritty Dorchester neighborhoods back home. First thing we did was kick off our sneakers, dig our feet into the cool powdery white sand and breath in the salt air. Is there any place on earth that smells better than the ocean? If there is, I haven't found it yet.

We'd build a bonfire then sit and talk for hours. I couldn't tell you what about, but I'm sure it centered around things like trying to get laid, what kid in school annoyed us the most, trying to get laid, Boston sports, trying to get laid, and getting drunk. You know, important shit like that. Did I mention trying to get laid? We all tried, but none of us did. We had *zero* game with the ladies. We'd pull our shirts back to try and make our chests look bigger or punch at our forearms to help them swell up thinking girls would like more muscular guys.

But it didn't help.

Nothing helped.

Joe twisted a beer and snapped the flying cap towards Beef. He ducked and tried to return fire but failed miserably.

"You know, kid, maybe if you didn't slice capicola all day, your hands wouldn't be so slimy," Kevin told him.

"It's sweat. You guys know I have a gland problem," Beef replied. "Besides, I'm not gonna work in that Deli forever."

"Great. You'll be the first one in your family not to smell like cold cuts," Joe said. (It's true. The whole family literally smelled like lunch meat all the time.)

As Beef jumped up to wash off in the ocean, Jimmy turned to Joe.

"You had to give him that nickname?"

"It's an homage," Joe replied. Not too many guys can smile 'ironically.' Joe was one of those guys.

"Watch out, Beef!" I yelled as he kneeled at the shoreline. "That girl in 'Jaws' went in the water at night, and she ended up as a hand."

"With crabs!" Joe added.

This caused Kevin to laugh out loud and I immediately thought to myself, 'Shit, I should have said that.'

There was always a hint of jealously for Kevin's affection. If you said a line he liked or, better yet, he laughed at, you were King for the night. Joe was the funny one. Beef got the sympathy nod because he was basically a child and Kevin figured he needed a nod every now and then. Jimmy got 'the nod' because, well because he was *Jimmy*.

But not me. I never got the 'Kevin Sullivan nod of approval.'

I snapped my beer cap at Beef.

"Stop, you guys. Leave Stevie alone," Katie said.

Katie always refused to call him Beef. In fact, I think Katie was the only person in Dorchester to call Steven by his given name. Even his parents and the teachers started calling Steve Beef. Everyone did. Well, everyone except Mrs. Callahan who always referred to him as *'that'* Steven, as in 'you're not going out with *that* Steven are you?'

Beef would turn bright red and smile like a smitten child every time Katie said his name. In fact, everyone in the neighborhood loved Katie Fitzgerald. She was beautiful and cool and basically untouchable, not just because she was Kevin's girl and he would kick your ass if you ever approached her, but because most guys didn't think they were good enough for her. It was almost as if Katie and Kevin were supposed to be together, you know? Like the neighborhood forced the relationship. Tough football star. Beautiful cool girl. It was just expected. But girls like Katie were never told what to do.

Kevin may have owned the football fields all over Boston, but Katie owned the hearts of every teenage boy in Dorchester.

Especially mine.

Truth be told, I had a silent crush on Katie since 8th grade. I didn't dare tell the guys. No one knew. But Katie and I had a connection. Sometimes we would even finish each other's sentences. We liked the same movies and TV shows. We had the same taste in music. In fact, I liked the Boz Scaggs *Silk Degrees* album, but I'd never admit that to Kevin. And although I didn't know it that night at the bonfire, we shared the same dreams and aspirations.

"What was it your dad used to say about saltwater?" Kevin asked Jimmy as he sat poking at the fire. "Washes everything away?"

"Washes away all your pain" Jimmy replied, the flames glowing on his face. "There's something about the ocean. It heals everything."

Jimmy stared out at Lewis Bay for a moment, then turned to the group. "Alright, fellow Norsemen. You guys bring your 'Offerings'?"

"C'mon, Jim," I said. "Seriously? We're really gonna do this?"

"A promise is a promise. Do it," Kevin snapped. His word was pretty much law with this group.

The night before Graduation Jimmy talked us into this 'Offering' thing, so we all brought something important along. Personally, I couldn't wait to remove all traces of Boston from my life, so I reached into my back pocket and tossed my diploma into the fire.

"So long, boys," I said. "Goodbye high school. Goodbye Dorchester."

"Those college girls better look out, huh Mikey?" Beef said enthusiastically and then slapped me five.

"You're so determined to get out of here, aren't you?" Kevin said to me.

"There's a whole world out there beyond Dot Ave, Kev," I replied.

"Keep it," he said, and the sad thing was we could all tell he meant it.

Kevin wasn't going anywhere.

My eyes met Katie's above the flames, and for a moment I thought I saw something. Jealousy? Regret? Did she want me to stay in Dorchester? Did she feel the same way about me? We both looked away before Kevin noticed.

Beef's turn.

He reached into his pocket and removed a Snickers bar he always kept 'for emergencies' and tossed it into the fire.

"Bet I start losing weight now," he said enthusiastically. We unanimously shot him enthusiastic 'thumbs up' signs and pantomimed support.

"Absolutely!" "You bet!" "Oh my God, of course!"

We were such assholes.

"So, this is what you guys do on these road trips?" Katie asked with biting sarcasm.

"I told you she wouldn't understand," Kevin said. "Chicks don't get it."

Katie punched him on the arm. Hard. Kevin tried not to wince, but you could tell she got him with a good one. Katie may look sweet, her green eyes bright and full, a spray of freckles across her nose, but she was city-tough to the core.

Jimmy looked at Joe, indicating that it was his turn.

Joe reached in his pocket and unfolded a letter from BERKLEE COLLEGE OF MUSIC.

"I got in," he said.

"That's awesome, Joe," Beef said.

Everything was awesome to Beef.

"Yeah, well, my Dad won't pay for some 'Goddamn long-haired hippie school,'" Joe said in a low grumble like his father would. "It's Holy Cross, then BC Law. Just like him. And his father. And everyone else in my family."

"You don't have to be them, Joe," Jimmy said, hoping that might help. It didn't.

"I know, but...I can't disappoint my dad," Joe said reluctantly, then we watched as he tossed the letter into the bonfire. "Rock and fucking roll, right?"

"Well, at least you and Kevin will be together," Beef said trying to cheer him up.

"I'm not going," Kevin said flatly.

"What!?" Jimmy said in shock.

"I turned Holy Cross down. I'm going to Curry," he said.

Jimmy looked to Kate, who was equally shocked.

"Did you know about this?"

"No. When did this happen?" she said, clearly pissed off.

Kevin didn't answer.

"Jeeze. Isn't your dad gonna be really mad?" Beef asked.

All eyes were on Kevin.

"My father doesn't give a shit what I do," he said, and we could all feel the hurt in his voice.

Parents were a mystery to all of us. Fathers especially. They were the guys who left the house at the beginning of the day and showed up some time around dinner. Mothers cooked the food and magically made dirty clothes reappear in the drawers of your room.

Joe's Dad was fairly successful. He had a cushy Government job through his Holy Cross and Boston College connections, and he made damn sure Joe was going to do the same.

My dad worked for the Boston Globe as a machine operator and always seemed too busy or too tired or too engrossed in the current sporting event on TV to really care about what I was doing.

Beef got along with his dad, mostly because he gave him free reign over the candy aisle at the Deli.

Jimmy's dad was the best. Mr. Callahan was the most approachable adult. You could talk and joke with him about anything, whether it was piling us into their Country Squire station wagon and driving to a Red Sox game or heading to Carson Beach on hot summer days, you always knew you were going to have fun. He would tell stories of how he lost his pinky working in a factory as a teenager, then stick the stub up his nose in a crowd. Or loudly sing 'I love to go swimming with bow legged women and swim between their legs.'

He was Jimmy's dad, but he belonged to all of us – me, Kevin, Joe, Beef – and Jimmy was happy to share him.

When he died, we were all devasted.

Kevin was right when he said his father didn't give a shit. For all his accomplishments on the football field, and there were a lot, Kevin's father never saw one game. Tommy Sullivan was a drinker. The MVP in a neighborhood of champion drinkers. He would go on binges, and combined with his hair-trigger temper, it made for a combustible homelife. Mr. Sullivan could turn into a pissed-off drunken rage at any second. He was a simmering pot always about to boil.

We used to see him outside his garage in the mornings on our way to school. We walked. No busses or family friendly carpools back then. Mr. Sullivan would be out front, holding a mug of coffee between his hands. He never waved or yelled out. He just watched us walk by. Joe was the first one to notice how in the dead of winter when it was maybe thirty degrees outside, there was never any steam coming off that hot cup of 'coffee.' We never said anything

27

to Kevin. We didn't want to upset him. Kevin's go-to excuse was that his father was always working at the garage, but we all knew 'Sully' was tipping it back at The Banshee.

When you grow up that way, always making excuses for your dad, you get a lot of anger – anger Kevin took out on the opponents roaming the football fields, or on anyone who made the mistake of teasing his frail best friend Jimmy Callahan.

Kevin draped an arm around Jimmy and looked at the bonfire.

"You think I'd leave you all alone back here in Dorchester, Jim? No way, kid. I'm gonna commute to Curry. We can do breakfast every mornin' at Linda Mae's, and hit the Eire Pub at night. Once I sign with the Pats, I'll buy a triple decker. Me and Kate on the first floor, you guys can rent above us."

"You're an asshole," Jimmy said through gritted teeth. I'd never seen him so mad.

Joe looked at Katie across the fire.

"Well, Miss Fitzgerald, any more surprises? You staying home too?"

"What? No. I don't know," she said, seething. "Well, I know my Offering."

Her eyes shot daggers at Kevin as she peeled off his football jacket and threw it in the fire.

"What are you doing? Are you crazy?! I gave that to you Freshman year!" Kevin shouted. But it was too late, the jacket was already burning.

"Jesus, he keeps everything," Joe whispered to Beef.

The tension was thick.

It was Kevin's turn, so I turned to him.

"Alright. Come on, asshole, time to give it up."

"What? Beef only tossed in a Snickers bar for Chrissake," Kevin replied.

"Hey, we all said we'd burn something meaningful. There's nothing more meaningful to me than chocolate," Beef admitted.

After a moment, Kevin leaned forward and pulled a worn Led Zeppelin 8-track from his back pocket. He stared at it for what seemed like eternity, then finally, reluctantly, tossed it into the fire.

"Happy now?" he said to Jimmy. "You and your Viking shit."

"They were warriors, Kev. Brothers like us. Lived life their own way. By their own code," Jimmy said, then he opened his gaze to us all. "The 'Offering' was whatever they felt was meaningful. Something to honor their friendship. But you want to know the coolest part? When someone died, they'd put the body in a boat, cover it with sticks, then just as the sun was setting, they'd light it on fire and push him off into the water."

Then Jimmy did something strange and wonderful. It's hard to describe, but he kind of looked right through us to the ocean, like he was looking beyond to something beautiful and perfect. Like this moment.

"The color of the flames and the color of the sky would melt into one. A symbol that the Viking had led a good life...and he would finally be at peace out there on the ocean."

Everything was perfectly clear to him, and perfectly right.

"'It's better to burn out, than to fade away,'" Joe sang. See what I mean? Neil Young. God, Joe was so cool.

"So, what are you gonna burn, Jimmy?" Beef asked. "Not the Fisk bat. You said it's worth money."

"Don't be an idiot, Beef. His father gave him that," Kevin said.

The five of us looked at each other, knowing it was a sensitive subject for Jimmy.

"Game six. Carlton Fisk at the plate," Jimmy said holding the baseball bat he took from Ronan now firmly in his hands.

"There it goes... long drive... If it stays fair... Home Run! There will be a Game 7!" Jimmy said imitating Dick Stockton's famous play-by-play. "It's the bat that almost won the Sox the Series, boys."

"Shouldn't that be in Cooperstown or something?" I asked.

"Should be, but it aint," Jimmy said. "My dad used to say, 'No way Carlton wants this stuck behind some glass case. In New York of all places. No. I brought something else."

Jimmy reached into his pocket and pulled out two rectangle pieces of paper. He stared at them for a moment, then let them fall from his hand and into the fire. We all knew what they were, but no one said anything. We just watched as a pair of unused Red Sox tickets curled and burned in the flames.

"We were doin' okay, my mother and me," Jimmy said, doing his teenage best to hold in the anger and the hurt and the sadness. "I mean, I know she was sad after my dad died and everything, but...she didn't have to go fuckin' marry *him.*"

Jimmy slowly pulled back the sleeve of his Barracuda jacket and revealed a white bandage on his forearm. As he peeled back the gauze, we all looked at a blistering bright red Celtic cross scar glistening underneath a gob of Vaseline.

"I knocked over his beer, so he had the redheads hold be down," Jimmy painfully admitted. "He fucking branded me."

Katie wiped away a tear.

Kevin looked like he was about to hop into the Love Boat, tare ass back to Dorchester and beat the living shit outta all the McShanes. Jimmy just gave him a look, a resigned one that seemed to say, 'it's useless.' Then he stood up and slowly approached the water's edge.

We all loved the Cape, but Jimmy found his only calm here.

"God, I love this place," he said, breathing the salt air deep into his lungs. "Promise me we'll always do this."

"Always do what?" Beef asked.

"This. All of us together. The Cape. The Love Boat. Everything."

We looked around and nodded. Everything was there and around us. We knew exactly who we were and exactly where we were going in life.

Jimmy turned to us, the flames from the bonfire reflecting off his face.

"You have one good friend you're lucky. Us? We hit the Goddamn lottery," he said, then yelled to the sky, "Norsemen!"

We all raised a beer and joined in.

"Norsemen!"

I thought everything changed in 1981.

It didn't.

Everything changed eighteen years later.

A hand slides an 8-track cassette into the car stereo.

Music blares from the speakers.

"Are you there?
Say a prayer for the Pretender
Who started out so young and strong
Only to surrender"

-Jackson Browne

CLEVELAND, OHIO - Eighteen years later

Lights flicker on the exhibits as the Rock and Roll Hall of Fame opens for the day.

Displays come to life. ABBA's costumes. Buddy Holly's glasses. Stevie Wonder's harmonica. Jim Morrison's Last Will and Testament. Elvis Costello's glasses.

A pale, gaunt, man in his thirties wearing a wrinkled janitors uniform stares up at a 'GREETINGS FROM CAPE COD' postcard taped to the inside of his locker.

Heroin is dumped into a spoon.

A match is struck. It brings the contents of the spoon to boil.

Tubing is wrapped around a skinny white arm.

A needle inhales the contents from the spoon.

The needle is inserted into a vein.

The man smiles and leans back against the locker.

Something is wrong.

He shakes, convulses and slumps.

The needle falls to the ground.

A thin, white forearm dangles revealing a branded Celtic cross.

DORCHESTER, MA - 1999

Sullivan Auto is a drab concrete block garage, part auto repair shop, part Boston sports shrine. Posters of past icons Bobby Orr, John Havlicek, Carl Yastremski, and Steve Grogan cover the walls.

Kevin Sullivan has aged a bit over the years, but the toughness still resonates in his manner. He turned the engine off and grabbed the worn vinyl case covered 70's Rock band stickers (The Clash. Led Zeppelin. Rolling Stones) beside him on the front seat.

His son Billy is the spitting image of his old man when he was eighteen. Ripped. Tough. His whole life in front of him.

Billy was rocking out to loud music when Kevin abruptly yanked the 8-track tape out of the stereo.

Billy jumped. He knows what's coming.

"I know, I know," Billy said. He's been through this routine before. "'Don't touch the tapes.' I get it. Just get an iPod, will ya bro?"

Kevin's face grimaced with pain. Bro?!

"Or at least use the CD player," Billy said.

"You mean like these?" Kevin said, reaching for a handful of Compact Discs. "This is your generation's version of *mixtapes*," he said as though the two words caused him to be physically ill.

"I hate *'mixtapes*. Let's see what you have here," Kevin said as he began to read the titles and dramatically drop each

36

CD to the shop floor. "'Afternoon Jams'. 'Afternoon Jams 2'. 'Acoustic Afternoon Jams.' 'Pregame Mix.' 'Party Mix 1'. 'Party Mix 2.' 'Party Mix 3.' 'RAGE'! 'Rage On'! 'Rage-Ing!' 'Totally Raging'! And...Sunday Morning Acoustic Hangover.'"

Kevin realized he'd gone a bit too far.

"Just...just don't touch my stuff, okay? And I'm not obsessed!"

"Sure, still driving the Love Machine and listening to 8-tracks," Billy scoffed. "Perfectly normal."

"Boat. It's the Love *Boat,*" Kevin snapped making sure Billy could hear the capital letters. "And those 8-tracks are classics."

"Ten songs to a tape and ten miles to a gallon. Now *that's* classic," Billy said, thick with sarcasm.

"Don't be a smart ass. Did you call the coach from Holy Cross back yet?"

Billy plopped his headphones back on, letting Kevin know that he is done with this conversation.

"He called the house three times already!" Kevin called out.

"Since when did you start givin' a shit?" Billy replied never looking up.

The words sounded familiar to Kevin.

"I just...I don't want you making the same mistake I did. Trust me, I know how a bad decision can affect the rest of your life," Kevin said without thinking, and immediately regretted saying that.

"Yeah, well, you didn't go to college and you turned out alright," Billy replied.

"Oh yeah, I hit the Goddamn lottery," Kevin said, more to himself than his son.

Kevin did hit the lottery once, sort of. The athletic lottery. Kevin Sullivan was the football pride of Dorchester. The slaps on the back. The free sandwiches at the Deli. The happy smiles and 'Good luck Friday night, kid,' greetings from everyone in the neighborhood. Kevin had it all.

And he knows how quickly it all disappears. Suddenly, you're just another kid from Dot Ave. Your father dies at fifty-eight from too much booze and anger. Your wife leaves you because she can see that you're turning bitter like your old man. You end up spending long days that bleed into others where Sundays don't feel much different than Tuesdays, catching a soft afternoon beer buzz, sitting around talking about the old days.

It's not the happy memories of Friday night football games that you carry back home.

It's the anger.

Kevin tried again to connect.

"Maybe you and I could drive out to Worcester, meet with the AD and..."

But Billy still wasn't listening.

"Somebody named Katie called before," he said offhandedly.

"Katie? Katie *Fitzgerald?*" Kevin asked a bit too eagerly.

"She said Crowley."

Kevin thought for a minute, then reached for the telephone and pushed the buttons. Yep, Kevin still had a push button phone. He might be the only person in Massachusetts (possibly the United States) who still has one. He fought the telephone company for months when they told him the analog rotary dials were obsolete. Kevin Sullivan really doesn't like change.

He waited for someone to pick up on the other end and grumbled, "*You kids today?* Christ listen to me...Hey, Kate.... It's...it's me. Kev."

Kevin listened for a moment, and his face gradually fell with the gravity of the news. Visibly shaken, he dropped the phone back into the cradle and paused to take it all in.

He picked up an 8-track cassette and fired it across the garage. It *CRASHED* against the wall and fell to the ground, splintering into pieces.

A hand slides an 8-track cassette into the car stereo.

Music blares from the speakers.

"Every time when I look in the mirror
All these lines on my face getting clearer
The past is gone
It went by, like dusk to dawn
Isn't that the way
Everybody's got the dues in life to pay"

-Aerosmith

DORCHESTER, MA

Every Saturday morning the four of us would be outside Beef's house waiting for him, listening as he sang along with Bugs Bunny cartoons on TV.

"Overture. Curtain lights. This is it. We'll hit the heights. And Oh what heights we'll hit. On with the show this is it."

We were always waiting for Beef.

We'd be getting pissed, about to leave, and then sure enough he would come bouncing out of the house with a handful of Blow pops or Razzles or a bag of Doritos.

"Sorry I'm late, guys," he'd say, oblivious to our sour moods. "I got you some stuff from the Deli."

I mean, Jesus Christ, how can you get mad at a kid like that? It's infuriating. My mother used to say Beef was 'a few French fries short of a happy meal.' He is bit dim, but Beef has a heart of pure gold. It's a fatal combination if you asked me.

Kevin sat behind the wheel of the Love Boat, his mood souring as he waited for Beef, just like when we were kids. He scanned the empty streets. No kids were playing anywhere. 'Look at this shit,' Kevin thought to himself. Beautiful Saturday like this we'd all be out of the house by nine o'clock the latest. Street hockey in the Fall and Winter, wiffleball in the Spring and Summer. God, we loved wiffleball. It's a shame that there's a whole generation of kids who won't grow up knowing the humiliation of a called third strike from a swooping knuckle-curve as it barely clinks off the corner of the lawn chair backstop.

Kevin smiled to himself, remembering those long easy days that floated into long easy nights, playing until the streetlights came on signaling it was time to go home. Christ, it all went by fast.

People walked past his car, heads down texting, earplugs in. Everything to Kevin was fast and new and shiny and loud. Everyone else was getting along in the world. Moving with it. Upgrading. Keeping up. When the fuck did that start happening? When did the pace suddenly pick up and leave him staring at everyone's back? As Kevin sat in the car waiting on his old friend, he felt like he was disappearing.

He'd waited long enough and was losing patience, so Kevin leaned on the horn. Beef waved to him from the Deli, looking disheveled, as always. His shirt was a stained mess of sweat and deli meats. A cool draft stood his thinning hair on end as he bent down to hug his five 'husky' kids goodbye. The youngest child, Anthony, wiped a smudge of chocolate from the side of his dad's mouth, and Beef laughed hard. Beef has a hearty, infectious laugh that bubbles up and bursts out of his jolly red face making it impossible for Kevin not to smile.

See what I mean? You can't *not* love this guy.

"I made you a sandwich for the ride," Beef said approaching the car. "My 10-inch Beef special."

"You don't think, maybe, you should change the name of that?" Kevin asked.

"No, why?" Beef replied, oblivious as always.

Beef grabbed the passenger door handle, but stopped, realizing he was about to take Jimmy's seat. Kevin waved him in, as if to say, 'Okay, just this once.'

"How do you do that?" Kevin asked as Beef climbed in the front.

"Do what?"

"Get your kids to like you."

Beef just shrugged and finished his half-eaten Snickers.

"Jesus, you're a sweaty mess," Kevin snapped.

"Red Sox lost again."

"You sweat *watching* a baseball game?"

Beef wiped his glistening brow with a handkerchief. You see, Beef has a gland problem that causes him to sweat. Like, all the time. We used to tease him about it, saying he's the only kid who could sweat while swimming. (Joe's line, not mine). It was always a waiting game to see when his armpit stains would expand and eventually meet in the middle.

"My minivan done yet?" Beef asked, his mouth full of chocolate.

"No, it's still in the garage" Kevin replied, losing patience. "And don't get any of that chocolate on the dash."

"I didn't," Beef said quickly wiping the brown smudge off before Kevin noticed and went ballistic. These two are like some bickering old married couple who have been stuck together for years.

    Kevin shifted the Love Boat into drive and peeled out, causing Beef's whole body to jerk backwards into the seat.

LOGAN AIRPORT

My flight from LAX to Boston arrived early, so I stopped by the airport bookstore. To my surprise, there was a table by the register with a display of my books. The sign read: From the author who gave you 'LEAD LIKE A VIKING: ANCIENT VIRTUES TO GUIDE LIFE THROUGH MODERN TIMES' - *GIMME 5! MIKE CROWLEY'S 5 POINT PLAN FOR SUCCESS*.

Unfortunately, that wasn't my only surprise. I would be lying if I told you sales were great. They weren't. They sucked. My books were piled high on a discount table. A fucking *discount* table!

The '90's were all about selling shit. Thighmasters. George Forman Grills. Sleeved blankets. People buy crazy shit from crazy people all the time. Sham Wow can wash a whole car. Knives can cut through a can. Why not a better-than-magic-beans 5 Point guide to bettering your life, right? Stick the words 'HOW TO' in front of it and people will flock to buy it. Thanks to insomnia and late shifts, people watched my 3:00 AM infomercials and made me a fortune. Then, Oprah recommended my book on her talk show and I became an instant celebrity. Every A-List actor signed up for my *GIMME 5!* technique.

Hey, I know my books are shit, but they sell. Or at least they used to. I called my editor.

"99 cents!?" I yelled into the always-glued-to-my-ear cell phone. "Yeah, I'm looking at them right now. What? I don't know, I'm meeting with the lawyers on Friday. I'm waiting for her to sign the..."

And that's when Beef mauled me with a bear hug, a little longer than I was comfortable being hugged. Kevin stood back and looked me up and down.

"There he is," he said. "Mister '5 Point Plan' himself. Best hair and teeth money can buy. Can't believe you actually showed up."

"Well, here I am," I replied, just as curt and as cold as he was.

"How's the left coast, Mikey?" Beef asked, oblivious to the tension between me and Kevin.

"You'd hate it Beef, everyone's a vegetarian," I said.

Kevin and I shook, and he squeezed my un-calloused, manicured hand, trying his best to piss me off. That always bothered my father too. He used to say, 'Never trust a man without callouses.' My father worked Monday through Saturday at the Globe, then spent all day Sunday working around the house fixing broken doors, painting rooms, repairing appliances. He had no patience or respect for a man who didn't know the difference between a Phillips head, or a Flat head, or a Torx, or a Pozidrv. I mean, who the fuck knew there were so many types of screwdrivers? Is it so bad that I'm successful and pay for landscapers and painters and handymen? That's Catholic Guilt for ya. Always in there ready to rear its ugly head whenever you're feeling too good about your own success.

"Still turning wrenches?" I asked Kevin, trying to match the strength of his grip.

"Still full of shit?" he replied, equally straining.

The tension between us broke when Joe jumped on Beef's back, surprising us all.

"Beefy Boy!"

We hadn't seen each other in years so it was finally a warm, heartfelt reunion. Joe looked great. Sharp suit, expensive tie, looking exactly like the corporate DC lawyer he'd become. We all knew he was the kid who'd go to college and make something of himself.

"Where's Katie?" Joe asked me.

"Oh, ah, she's coming out later," I deflected, not ready to get into all that just yet. "We're having some trouble with the pool."

"You have a pool?!" Beef asked.

"Pool and a pond," Joe recited. "Pond would be good for you."

Guys our age never miss a chance to quote Caddyshack. This line was a lay-up.

We grabbed our luggage and wheeled it out to the parking lot.

****

"Oh my God. *Thar she blows!*" Joe yelled when he spied the enormous Bonneville looking like a whale among a school of minnows.

I turned to Kevin. "You're still driving the Love Boat?"

"Yep. Only sixty thousand miles on this bad boy," he said proudly. "Just down the Cape and back. All highway, baby."

I glanced inside at the odometer. Yep. 62,438. The car was in mint condition. Probably looked better than the day Kevin's grandfather bought it. Kevin did his best 'Isaac the Bartender' finger point, then popped the trunk. I had forgotten that he removed the spare tire and the jack and converted the whole space into a cooler. Joe looked down at the beer-filled trunk.

"I can't believe General Motors hasn't made this part of their 'functional alcoholic' package."

"It does come in handy," Kevin replied with a smirk.

Beef reached for the front passenger door handle and Joe and I immediately looked at each other.

"It's okay," Kevin spoke up. "I told him he could."

"Well, welcome back to 1981 boys," Joe said climbing into the back and spotting Kevin's precious vinyl case of 8-tracks.

"Jesus. You still have these?" I said.

"Don't fuck with those tapes," Kevin snapped from the driver's seat. "They're all in--"

"--alphabetical order."

We know. We all finished the sentence for him.

"Have you bought anything since the '80's? You should really get an iPod," I told him.

49

"So, I been told," Kevin growled.

"Mine holds 200 songs," I told him.

"Yeah? I didn't know Hall and Oates had 200 songs," Kevin laughed. "You know how many cars come into my shop because some idiot kid was fumbling to find the next song on those stupid iPoddy things? Not me. Watch."

Then Kevin's right hand roamed the vinyl case, hovering over each row and tape to prove his point.

"Three over, four down. 'The Doors.' Five over, two down. 'Led Zeppelin.' Row two, section two. 'Bad Company.' See, it's a fool-proof system," Kevin said proudly. "I never take my eyes off the road."

It was like some Classic Rock version of the game Battleship.

"Jeeze, it's good to have you guys home. Just like old times, right?" Beef said, then his voice trailed off. "Well...sort of."

We all knew what he was talking about.

Jimmy should be here.

Joe broke the silence. "So, we headin' down the Cape?"

"I told Mrs. Callahan we'd stop by when I got here," I said.

Kevin was pissed. "Christ almighty. Really?!"

"She hates me," Beef said. "I was always '*that*' Steven. How come it was never 'that' Michael, or 'that' Kevin? I'm not a 'that' kind of kid."

"Maybe she meant 'fat' kid," Kevin said with a smirk.

"I was husky!" Beef blurted out loud.

"So, Old Man McShane still sitting sentry on the front porch?" I asked trying to change the subject.

"He died, Mikey," Beef replied solemnly.

"Well, not so much died," Joe remarked. "More like he got hit over the head and stopped being alive."

Kevin raised his eyes and glared at me in the rear-view mirror. "Maybe if you called once in a while, you'd know that shit."

The car fell silent. Kevin just gripped the wheel tight and stared straight ahead.

I began to regret coming home.

Or at least it used to be home a lifetime ago.

****

The Love Boat pulled off Morrissey Boulevard and we entered the streets of Dorchester. I sat by the window and looked around at the old neighborhood. I used to know every occupant of every house. Everybody knew everybody back then. Now, most people from the old days have moved. They sold their triple-deckers to rich developers who pushed them out, gutted the building, and turned them into shiny new condos. I laughed to myself, thinking how those rich

Dorchester yuppies in their BMW's and Mercedes must look at Kevin's monster of a car and make sure they give it a wide berth when parking.

I suddenly felt old and out of place, like I didn't belong, and the guys were strangers to me. Years of practice let me shed the hometown Boston accent around the Hollywood elite. Sometimes, when I have too much to drink, the accent slips out. I drop my R's and say things like 'wicked pissah.' But for the most part I can turn it on and off like a charm. After high school, I shed this town like a bad page of writing. I wadded it up in my fist, tossed it aside and never looked back.

Mrs. Callahan's house was run down with age and neglect, but still had the white Irish lace curtains fluttering in the windows. The exterior was covered with chipped paint. The small patch of lawn out front was overgrown with weeds. Beer cans, whiskey nip bottles and cigarette butts littered the ground. It was almost as if she was proud of the house in disrepair, the way it taunted the yuppie-refurbished triple-deckers up and down the street as if to say, 'Screw all you invaders and the sellouts who took the money and bailed.'

Mrs. Callahan was old school Dorchester. Tough and proud, full of piss and vinegar. Or at least she used to be.

She opened the door wearing an Irish sweater buttoned over her flowered housecoat.

"Oh, boys. Come in," she said. "And wipe your feet. I don't want you kids getting dirt all over my new carpet."

It wasn't new.

Nothing in the house was new.

We entered a dark, tired, musty home that died years ago along with Mr. Callahan. Decay permeated the place.

A small bowl of holy water hung below a framed photo of Cardinal Cushing in the front hallway and Beef nervously blessed himself, as if that might help him stop sweating from fear.

It didn't.

Mrs. Callahan lit up when she saw me.

"There he is. Oh Michael, you've gotten even more handsome. Jesus, Mary and Joseph, wait till I tell the women at St. Bridget's that a movie star was here."

I could almost hear Kevin's eyeballs roll in their sockets

"It's just Goddamn infomercials," he muttered. Mrs. Callahan glared. She did not appreciate profanity, although she'd been known to throw a good one around when it was needed. I noticed how uncomfortable Kevin was in her presence. More than usual.

"Best of friends you all were," Mrs. Callahan said. "The Five Horsemen."

"Norsemen," Kevin corrected her. "The Five *Norsemen*. You remember, right Mike?"

But I didn't answer. I was too busy checking my cell phone, like always.

Mrs. Callahan turned to us.

"Look at you boys, so grown up and important. Just like my Jimmy. He had a very important job you know. At the Cleveland Music Conservatory. Such a good boy, he was. I tried to take care of him after his father died... I really did... I just..."

Her voice trailed off with sadness and confusion.

There was definitely something off. You could just tell she wasn't all *there,* you know? Maybe dementia. Maybe the years of abuse. Maybe the loss of her beloved son Jimmy. They were all taking their toll on the tired, sad old woman.

I looked at Mrs. Callahan and felt badly for her. There was something about the look on her face. It was a face full of hard-learned wisdom and hurt that she never asked for.

"Can we give you a ride to the church tomorrow, Mrs. Callahan?" I asked, trying to move the conversation along. I was anxious to get out of the house and out of Dorchester. Big time.

"Oh no, Michael, the funeral is Friday. Didn't Katie tell you? Jimmy is still in Ohio," Mrs. Callahan said.

"Friday?! But I thought..." I started, but Kevin jumped in.

"That's fine, Mrs. Callahan. We'll be there," he said.

Mrs. Callahan's eye's met Kevin's, and for the first time she seemed coherent and resolute.

"I know you will," she said firmly. "Jimmy could always count on you."

Kevin just sort of nodded and looked away.

"Mass will be at St. Mark's and burial at Holy Name," she continued.

"Holy Name? But, isn't Mr. Callahan buried at Saint Anne's in Braintree?" Beef asked nervously, the sweat beginning to pool in the creases of his neck.

Joe tried to help. "St. Anne's is on the way to the Cape. You know how Jimmy loved it when we'd all drive down there."

But Mrs. Callahan cut him off with the wave of her purple-veined hand.

"The McShane family has plots all paid in full. You know I don't have that kind of money. Jimmy will be home in a few days and Holy Name cemetery will be fine," she said as she looked off. "It...it will just have to be."

A hand slides an 8-track cassette into the car stereo.

Music blares from the speakers.

"Well, I woke up this morning,

I got myself a beer
The future's uncertain,

and the end is always near"

-The Doors

DORCHESTER, MA

The Banshee is a working-class bar with yellow stains on the wainscot ceiling and empty cases of beer bottles stacked like benches along the walls. It's the kind of place where locals come to nurse their alcoholism and regret and talk bullshit, filled with men who've made sitting on bar stools a profession. The beer is cheap and cold, and everyone minds their own business.

The four of us settled into a booth near the back.

"Are you shittin' me?" Joe said. "She's gonna bury him next to Old Man McShane?"

"It's not right," Beef replied with a sigh.

I glared at Kevin, more concerned about getting back home than about funerals and cemetery plots.

"Why did you have me get here so early? I have to be back in LA for a meeting on Friday."

Kevin didn't answer.

"This is great," Beef said with his child-like exuberance. "We can all hang out like old times. Besides, we have to wait for the car service to bring Jimmy home anyway, right?"

Kevin, who had been staring off, killed his beer and came back down to earth. He placed the bottle firmly on the table, then raised his eyes to meet us.

"That's not gonna happen."

"Excuse me?" I said.

"We're going to get him," Kevin said, widening his gaze to take us all in. We could tell by his look that he was serious.

I hadn't seen that look since high school. It was halftime of the Thanksgiving football game our Junior year. As we sat in the locker room, down two touchdowns, Kevin shot us all a look of fierce determination, and no one doubted him. That look all but guaranteed we would kick the shit out of Catholic Memorial.

The second half of the game was war. Kevin switched to tailback, scored three touchdowns and broke the school's all-time record for tackles on defense. We won by six.

Sitting there, looking at us in the bar, Kevin had that same fierce determination in his eye.

"You're not serious," I said.

"Come on. We were young and crazy once, let's be that way again. One more time. One last road trip. Honestly, we should have done something like this years ago," Kevin said before his tone turned more serious and pointed. "We're the ones who should bring Jimmy home. We made a promise."

"Oh sure, like when we all promised to get tattoos," Beef said looking to his hip where a poorly drawn yellow Tweety Bird sits inked on his pinky white skin. "I can't believe I went first," he muttered. (We all bailed on the idea of getting tattoos once Beef said it hurt.)

Joe spoke up.

"I don't know, Kev. I have to be in DC. My father's coming up from Florida for the ceremony and..."

"He never came to a Goddamn thing," Kevin snapped. "You think he's gonna start now?"

He was right and we all knew it.

Joe tugged at his tie. He looked tired. Tired of people. Tired of his clothes. Tired of office politics. Tired of the bullshit. His grin was answer enough, but he confirmed it by saying, "Let's do it."

I wasn't as excited.

"Don't you think we're getting a little old for this kind of nonsense?"

"Remember that time we stole Kelly's Crown Vic?" Beef said smiling at the memory. "Got halfway to the Sagamore before the police stopped us."

"We were making great time," Joe quipped.

"Jimmy took the blame for that whole thing," Beef said shaking his head sadly. "He never said a word."

"He took a real beatin' from McShane for that," Kevin added. "Took too much of everything from that prick."

No one knew what to say.

We never really talked about what went on behind those white Irish lace curtains in the Callahan house after Jimmy's father died. We just knew it was bad.

Unspeakably bad.

Like, 'you don't even want to know' bad.

"Was he really a janitor?" I asked breaking the silence.

"You mean, 'Vice President of Interior Organization for the Cleveland Music Conservatory,'" Beef said, doing his best imitation of Mrs. Callahan.

"More commonly known as the Rock and Roll Hall of Fame," Joe added.

"Well, Jimmy did love music," Beef said.

"And apparently disinfectant," Joe added.

"What the hell was he doing in Cleveland?" I asked.

Beef shook his head and looked at the bottles of beer lined on the table and said, "Scholarship to UMass. History Professor. Smartest guy in our high school without even trying."

"If he was so smart, then why did he OD?" I remarked without thinking.

The second I said that I wanted to take it back. But it was too late. The damage had been done.   Kevin bashed me with a look.

"You don't know that, Mike. In fact, you don't know a fuckin' thing."

There was a hard, awkward silence. Even the old gents at the bar turned to see if everything was alright.

"I hadn't talked to Jimmy in a long time. I didn't realize he was so unhappy," Beef said, his voice barely above a whisper.

Joe looked at his watch and grumbled like Glum from the old Gulliver's Travels Saturday Morning cartoon.

"We'll never make it."

"We will if we leave first thing in the morning," Beef announced with a smile.

He was in   .

"We should probably tell our moms we're having a sleepover, so they won't be suspicious," Joe added sarcastically.

"Maybe it was just an accident," I said, still trying to recover from my insensitive overdose comment.

"Accident or suicide, it doesn't matter. Our friend is dead and we're the ones bringing him home. And you know what?" Kevin said, and a slow, shit eatin' grin toasted across his face. "Jimmy's gonna love every minute of it."

He was the high school linebacker again. Fearless. In charge. Seeing the whole field.

"Cleveland?" I asked. "Seriously?"

Kevin slammed his Cape Cod key chain on the table.

"Seriously."

Then he started to sing.

"Love....Exciting and new..."

Beef and Joe joined in.

"Come aboard...We're expecting you.... The Looove Boat."

As crazy and it sounds, we were all in.

A hand slides an 8-track cassette into the car stereo.

Music blares from the speakers.

"It's been a long time since I rock and rolled
It's been a long time since I did the Stroll

It's been a long time
been a long lonely, lonely, lonely, lonely, lonely time"

-Led Zeppelin

BOSTON POLICE STATION

Detective Richie Kelly was a local product brought up on the streets of St. Greg's Parish in Dorchester. He was an old school Boston Detective, which basically meant he had high blood pressure, a bad diet, and a lifetime of blown relationships. The blood pressure situation wasn't helped by the fact that his immediate superior was Kim Bletzer, a powerful take-no-bullshit African American. Not only did Kelly have to report to a *woman*, he had to report to a woman that he trained. And to make matters worse, he worked with Kim's father Curt back in the day, a beat cop who retired on a disability and moved to the Martha's Vineyard. The lucky prick.

Kim married into a family of lawyers, one of which, the father-in-law, was a judge. Pretty high level given how fast Kim rose through the department. Kim had the brains, work ethic and attitude that was respected by her fellow officers, but most of all Kim Bletzer didn't take shit from any of the 'good old boys.' She could handle her way around guys like Richie Kelly whose big mouth, short temper, and unfiltered remarks kept him from being promoted in today's politically correct environment. In hushed tones, Richie would tell close friends that he didn't get promoted because he had the '2-P's' working against him: Pigment and Penis.

Kim entered the office with a thick manila folder tucked under her arm.

"You want I should stand and salute?" Kelly asked, chock full of attitude.

"Let's try and be civil here, Richie," Bletzer replied.

"Sure. Thirty years on the force and I get to call the kid I trained, and whose *father* I trained, my boss. Great. How can I help... Ma'am?"

"Twenty-nine years and *eight months* on the force," she snapped back. "You're not retired yet, old man. You want to spend these last few months with Human Resources taking Sensitivity Training?"

"I'd rather work with the crack heads," he muttered under his breath.

"You want to explain to me why the McShane case is still open?" Bletzer demanded. "Really shouldn't be this hard."

This particular case bothered her. Bletzer knew Richie Kelly had the highest solve rate in the unit. There had to be a reason he was dragging his feet.

She opened the folder and scanned the Coroner's report.

"Bludgeoning. That says rage to me. That says out of control and messy, not a contract hit," Bletzer said raising her eyes to meet Kelly. "This attack wasn't random, you do know that, right?"

Kelly leaned back in his chair his hands laced behind his head.

"Lotsa houses in Dorchester," he replied full of the arrogance and superiority that almost 30 years on the job gave him. "Most of them triple-deckers. That's a lot of people to interview. It's takin' a while. But, you're from Milton, right?

You probably don't get that people around here don't really line up to cooperate with the police."

Kim Bletzer thought for a moment before speaking.

"Look, Richie, I know you have history with this one. 'Dot Rats.' 'Protect your own' and all that bullshit. Different times now. It's all about reports and crime rates and stats. If you want off, let me know. I'll reassign you and you can ease into retirement, but I'm getting heat on this one. Some developer is looking at the Navy Yard. Wants to build condos or some shit, like everywhere else. They don't need an open murder case on record."

Bletzer dropped the folder onto his desk.

"Just make it go away."

Kelly did his best not to check out her ass as she left, then turned his attention to the Coroner's report.

He had nothing. He didn't have a witness. He didn't have a murder weapon. He didn't have any evidence. What he did have was a gut feeling. The kind that twenty-nine years and eight months on the job gives you.

Kelly leaned forward and grabbed an autographed baseball that sat on the corner of his desk and slowly began to spin it in his hand.

It's not that Richie Kelly wasn't doing his job. He was better at it than most. It was more than that. This case was personal.

More personal than he wanted to admit.

BEEF'S DELI

Beef was far too trusting for this world. Innocent and always eager to help. "Be with you in a minute," he yelled out from behind the counter, wiping his hands with the damp towel he'd been using to clean the stainless-steel prep table. His face fell when he saw Corey McShane enter his neighborhood corner store. The McShanes never used the front like the real customers, they came through a side door that opened onto the alley.

Corey strolled in casually and pushed Beef aside with an air of bully toughness. He reached into the cooler for a slab of roast beef and tossed it onto the slicer.

"Me grandad was a butcher back home," he said as he fired up the meat slicer and menacingly began to cut himself thin slices of the juicy red meat. "Us McShanes...I think we like to cut things up. Between Jimmy's love of the smack and your keen sense of pickin' losers, you Yanks have been good for business. That is, 'till one of youse up and dies...like Jimmy."

He turned and looked directly at Beef.

"You're in the hole, fat man," he said grabbing a handful of the sliced roast beef. "A pretty fuckin' deep one."

Then Corey spun and wailed the sliced meat at Beef. He ducked at the last minute. It was as if all those years of snapping beers caps at Beef's head trained him for that moment. The meat *SLAPPED* against the wall, the blood red juice running down the concrete.

"I...I just need a little more time," Beef said, frozen with fear.

Corey grabbed a plastic wiffleball bat from a nearby display and pinned it to Beef's sweaty neck.

"Look, this ain't no, 'good cop-bad cop' here, boyo. It's all bad cop. But I'm the sane one of the bunch. Got that from me mother's side. Me brother? Not so much," Corey said, then his eyes glanced at the roast beef still clinging to the wall. "He's gonna want his pound of flesh."

Beef, now glistening with sweat, looked at the yellow plastic bat held to his neck. And he got an idea.

"I...I think I know how I can get the money."

Corey placed his index finger against Beef's forehead, cocked his thumb and held it there for what probably seemed like hours. Then he dropped the hammer, took his finger back and blew on it like some bullshit make-believe Gangster.

"I'm sure you will, lad," Corey smiled condescendingly. "I'm sure you will."

That's when I came into the store.

Corey walked past, eyeing me up and down, and casually mocked, "*GIMME 5!* brother!"

I just looked at Beef, who was now a soaked, sweaty mess.

"You really should see someone about this gland thing. Come on, we gotta Rock n' Roll. The guys are waiting."

A hand slides an 8-track cassette into the car stereo.
Music blares from the speakers.

"And I'll be taking care of business every day
Taking care of business every way
I've been taking care of business it's all mine
Taking care of business

And working overtime"

-Bachman Turner Overdrive

Beef leaned out the window so far that I couldn't believe he didn't fall out. He pumped his arms, screamed, "Rock and Roll!" and then struggled to get his burly frame back into the car.

Joe lifted the Pioneer speaker covers from the back dash and reached directly into the trunk. Only this time, it wasn't for beers. Joe pulled out Pepto Bismol for Beef, a Red Bull for Kevin, Metamucil for himself, and a protein shake for me.

It was all different.

Different bodies.

Different people.

Different road trip than when we were teenagers.

But we were genuinely excited to be together, although the reason for our trip really wasn't mentioned. I mean, we all knew we were heading out to get Jimmy, but after a while, we sort of settled into the idea and just tried to enjoy the ride.

As soon as we hit the Mass Pike headed west, Kevin slapped in one of his 'K-TEL PRESENTS TOP HIT'S OF THE 70's' 8-tracks. I'm not sure exactly what song it was that got us all going. Maybe 'Kung Fu Fighting' by Carl Douglas, or 'The Night Chicago Died' by Paper Lace, or 'Seasons in the Sun' by Terry Jacks - although I'm pretty sure I'd remember if it was 'Seasons in the Sun' because Beef always ended up crying by the end.

Jesus. Carl Douglas. Paper Lace. Terry Jacks. This quite possibly could be the Holy Trinity of One Hit Wonders.

73

The magical thing about 8-tracks was that the song would sometimes fade in mid verse. You'd be singing along at the top of your lungs and the song would suddenly fade out and stop. You'd all stare blankly in silence, then - CLICK - the track changed, the song began again, and everyone continued to sing along without missing a beat.

We drove along, belting out our 70's 'One Hit Wonder' (I'm pretty sure it was *Everybody was Kung-Fu Fighting*) when we heard even louder music approaching from behind. Turned out, it was carload of teenagers, their heads bouncing to their own loud music pumping from the speakers.

The irony wasn't lost on us.

I saw Kevin grin in the rear-view mirror. He slowed down to allow the cars to run side by side on the highway, then he looked over and angrily flipped the teenagers the finger.

Kevin hates todays music.

Like deep in his bones hate.

Most of all that 'Rap-crap' as he eloquently refers to it.

He hit the gas and the powerful V-8 engine of the Love Boat took off. I bet we were doing close to a hundred (thank God Beef was having too much fun to notice) and we left the Rap-crap-listening teenagers in the dust.

"Can we just put on the radio?" I asked innocently.

Joe and Beef looked at each other and shuddered with fear, knowing my request was about to set off a shit storm.

"Sure," Kevin replied as calmly as possible, almost singing the words to lure me in the way a cat plays with a mouse before killing it.

"What should we listen to?" he asked almost too nicely. "Pop? Oldies? Country and fuckin' Western? Ooh, I know. Top 40."

He was just revving up, like a pot about to boil.

"And who decides on that Top 40? The fucking record companies, that's who! Jamming Bubble Gum Pop shit down our throats. You buy the album, then *play* the album. Not just The Greatest Hits. All of it! Nobody listens to the B-side or the deep cuts anymore," Kevin argued to no one in particular.

I looked at Joe and mouthed, "B-side?"

"Forget it. He's rolling," he replied. (See what I mean? Guys our age *never* miss the opportunity to quote Animal House.)

Kevin continued his rant.

"Look at the album sleeve. Appreciate the art. Read the lyrics. Touch it. Feel it."

His anger was comical. I knew it was pointless to continue the conversation. It was Kevin's tapes or nothing.

He realized he'd gone too far.

Kevin drove for a bit, then tried to get his emotions under control and come back from Crazy Town.

"Anyway... *that's* why I hate the radio," he said, almost embarrassed.

"And *that's* why he's not with a woman," Joe whispered to Beef.

We all loved music, but Kevin took it to a whole other level. His music set the tone and was an important background for everything we did. It was as if our lives had their own daily soundtrack.

"Come on. You gotta admit, there are some good bands out there today," I added.

"Bands are like pizza places," Kevin said.

Me, Joe and Beef just looked at each other, thinking he really had gone crazy.

"Just hear me out," Kevin said. "There's no shortage of pizza places, right? I mean, there are a lot of average ones that look like all the others, and then there are ones that are definitely unique but are more concerned with their appearance than they are with making a good product. But the *best* ones...ah."

He put a finger to his lips like and old Italian Mama reminiscing about her favorite dish.

"You mean like Hi-Fi Pizza," Beef said, his mouth watering. "God, I miss that place. The best."

We all agreed. Hi-Fi made the best pizza in all of Dorchester. Maybe all of Boston. We were devasted when it closed. We all tried to find a better slice, but there's nothing like the original.

"It's like that with bands," Kevin continued. "The best ones are rare, instantly great, classic but not inauthentic. And you just want to keep going back to it, you know? And when it's gone, it's gone forever. You always miss it."

We sat on that for a bit. Missing places like Hi-Fi. Missing the innocence and fun of our youth. Missing everything.

"But not music, man," Kevin said cranking up the volume and staring at the road that lay ahead. "Music lasts forever."

We smiled and enjoyed the music as the Love Boat sped along going a smooth 80 miles-per-hour and the landscape started to get more rural.

We thought we had lost that carload of teenagers, but suddenly, they gained on us and pulled alongside. Before Kevin could flip them off again, Beef took it upon himself to mix things up. He unbuckled his pants, propped himself up, and jammed his pimply white ass against the window.

Kevin nearly swerved off the road, he was laughing so hard.

We all were.

I was starting to realize how much I missed these guys.

THE EIRE PUB – DORCHESTER, MA

The Eire Pub was the McShane's bar. Everyone knew it. The sign outside reads 'Men's Bar', but they might as well change it to 'McShane's.' The two stools at the far end belonged to Corey and Ronan, and God help you if you ever sat in one by mistake. The brothers sat slumped over two pints.

"So, when's the Goddamn funeral then?" Ronan growled.

"Friday," Corey replied.

"Christ almighty."

"A real shame."

"Fuck that," Ronan snapped. "The real shame is he owed us money. And you let him just skip town?!"

"What did you want me to do, drive to Cleveland?"

Ronan shot his brother a terrifying look.

"You're losin' yer balls…and yer identity. Look at yourself, for fuck sake," Ronan said, glaring at his brother dressed in some sort of urban rapper starter kit. A sideways flat brim hat. Gold chains. FUBU shirt. Baggy pants. Corey had somehow arrived at the misconception that he was black, and his fashion sense ran towards inner-city-rapper-wanna-be.

Ronan, the older twin by three minutes and dangerously psychotic, scanned the bar with disgust. Unlike Corey who had acclimated to the lifestyle and trends, Ronan hated all things American, especially the proliferation and exploitation of the Irish culture.

"It's this fuckin' country, made ye soft," he growled. "Stickin' shamrocks and leprechauns on everything. It don't make it Irish. Just like ploppin' a silly hat and gold chain round ye neck don't make ye fuckin' 'Gansta.'"

He took along pull on his Guinness, then asked, "You visit the Deli man like I told ye?"

Corey just nodded.

"And?"

"Close to twenty."

Ronan grimaced like it pained him.

"Jayzus. Let me tell you something, brother dear. Do you know why you don't kill a man who owes you five thousand dollars? Because you lose the opportunity for him to make good on the debt. But when that man rakes up ten, fifteen, *twenty*? Well, you know he'll never pay... so you need to make an example of him."

The bartender brought over another round. Corey hurriedly paid the tab, establishing the correct pecking order of brothers.

"That better not be a piss American beer you're drinkin' or someone's gonna lose an eye," Ronan growled staring straight ahead. Corey was lucky enough to have ordered a Smithwicks.

They both looked up at the baseball game playing on the television above the bar. Ronan had had just about enough.

"Would ye look at this American shite? Nobody tackles anybody. And the coach wears a fuckin' uniform. What's with thah'?"

"The Yanks are mad for the trinkets though," Corey replied. "That crazy as rat shit Charlie Sheen? Bought a ball once for over four hundred grand."

"And what's that got to do with you gettin' me fuckin' money?!" Ronan growled.

"You remember that bat of Jimmy's? Called it 'The Fisk Bat' or some shite? Could be worth a fortune to the right baseball lovin' 'eejit."

Ronan thought on that piece of information for a bit.

"Jayzus, I shoulda known. Carryn' it around in a fuckin' guitar case all the time. Fucker didn't even play. You know where it is then?"

"Nah, but the fat Deli man does," Corey replied.

Ronan reached for an Eire Pub cocktail napkin and wiped the Guinness foam from his lips.

A nasty grin inched across his face.

"Well brother, I think it's time we best remind them fuckin' Yanks who runs this town."

ROADSIDE DINER

We stopped somewhere on the New York, Pennsylvania border in a town that looked like every other town in the middle of the country. Bars. Gas stations. Strip malls. Closed mills and clothing factories. It was the kind of town where people are grateful for the seasons because it means time is actually moving on. All I knew is that we were a long way from my 10,000 square foot house on the water in Malibu.

We entered the Diner and Beef and I slid into a booth while Kevin and Joe made a beeline for the Jukebox. It was full of CD's, not records, which immediately set Kevin off. Joe fed a dollar in and started making selections when Kevin swiftly slapped his arm away as if Joe were trying to drown a puppy or something.

"Whoa, whoa, whoa. What the hell are you doing?" Kevin snapped.

"Playing some music," Joe replied, stunned.

"Playing *some* music? Do you have any idea what songs might come up? Do the research, for Chrissake. Pay attention to your investment. Don't take this so lightly."

"Oh God, here it comes," Joe said, his eyes rolling in their sockets.

Then Kevin began to instruct Joe like a father teaches his young son how to hit a baseball for the first time.

"Now, your first selection is critical. It's the one that usually comes on while you're still standing here making your other picks, so you need to make sure it's a good one. One that will make the crowd go, 'Hmmm, good pick my man.' You have a responsibility up here, Joe. You set the mood for the entire place. The first song in your rotation is key."

Joe just stood there listening.

"Personally, I like to go with an Allman Brothers or a Bob Marley as my leadoff hitter. They're staples. Every Juke box will have their greatest hits album. I usually hit them with number 11 on Marley's *Legend* Album 'Wait in Vain.' It's a nice, evenly paced reggae, and nobody *doesn't* like Marley. Plus, it lets you know who might be carrying some weed, ya know what I'm sayin'?"

"You're amazing," Joe replied, with the naïve face of a child.

"I haven't even started yet!" Kevin shot back. "Now, that buys me the time I need to stay up here and make my more unique and eclectic selections."

"Ooh, they have Marvin Gaye," Joe said, about to select a song.

Kevin slapped his hand away again.

"We're not marching against fuckin' Vietnam here, Joe. Pay attention! Now we go back to the Allman Brothers for your back-up. In my 3-hole is anything by The Stones *prior* to 1981. And batting clean-up?" His eyes scanned the CD's through the plexiglass. "Ah, beautiful. They have J Geils Band *Blow Your Face Out*. We're done. And now we can confidently join our party, relax and enjoy our meal while we await our musical medley without fear of shame or ridicule."

They joined us at the booth.

"He give you the 'Juke Box selection' speech," Beef asked Joe who just sort of nodded with the kind of stunned face you have if you just saw your parents having sex.

"This place is great," Beef chimed. Everything was great to Beef. He was like a grammar school kid on a field trip. "You think this place has a gift shop?"

Beef had been on a spending spree since we left Dorchester, buying souvenirs at every stop we made. Snow globes from the Mass Pike rest area. Maple syrup from Stockbridge. Shot glasses from Albany. The plastic bags were beginning to pile up.

The waitress approached our booth.

"What can I get you boys?"

"Boys? Well, aren't you sweet...Cheryl, is it?" I asked, checking her name tag. "What a beautiful place you have here."

I really poured it on. I know point Point One of my 'GIMME 5! Five Point Plan' is **Honesty**, but this place was disgusting. And besides, Cheryl ate it up. I find I get better service when I flirt.

"Do you have any Gluten free grass-fed organic items on your menu?" I asked trying my best not to be condescending.

But I was.

Thank God 'Dancing Queen' by ABBA suddenly started playing because I truly thought Kevin was going to kill me.

"The fuck is this?!" Kevin blurted. "The Juke Box broken or something?"

"I don't think so," Cheryl replied looking over. "Seems to be working just fine,"

"Well, I didn't play this fucking song!" Kevin snapped defensively.

"Take it easy, Kev. You really need to work on your anger," I said to him. "I use a Bikram yoga breathing technique that…"

Kevin shot me a 'shut the fuck up' look.

I shut up.

"See? This is exactly why you need a process," he groaned. "Now everyone thinks I'm a fuckin' ABBA fan."

Kevin slumped in the booth.

We all started singing just to piss Kevin off.

"You can dance. You can jive. Having the time of your life…"

Bustin' balls. Just like old times.

I was actually having a good time.

****

While we sang 'Dancing Queen' and ate our non-Gluten free non-grass-fed non-organic greasy food, Cheryl was back at the counter taking an order from two hunters, Ned and Chester.

How did I know Ned and Chester were hunters? Well, the flannel, the camouflage, and the dead dear I saw through the window tied to the hood of their truck in the parking lot were pretty good clues.

Ned, the bigger of the two, asked, "Juke Box broken?"

"There is nothing wrong with the Juke Box. Why does everyone keep asking that?" Cheryl replied.

"Then how did this crap music come on?" Ned snapped.

Cheryl rolled her eyes and looked in our direction.

"Ya know, that handsome one with the teenage girl appetite looks really familiar."

"You flirtin' again, Cheryl?" Ned snapped.

"We're through, Ned. Done. I kicked your ass out weeks ago, remember?! And stop having stuff delivered to my house. I got enough of your crap," Cheryl told him, then crouched below the counter and tossed a plastic Diner bag onto his lap.

"Careful with that!" Ned yelled, quickly checking the contents then he gently, *carefully* placed the bag by his feet.

"She'll take me back. You'll see," he said to his sidekick Chester, the mini version of Ned. Because of all the camouflage, you could have mistaken Chester for a small bush with a neon orange cap.

Ned's eyes narrowed as he turned his attention to the four of us singing and laughing in our booth.

It wasn't the ABBA song he hated so much.

It was Kevin's Patriot's jersey.

There's a long history of New York vs Boston sports rivalries. We used to be on even footing, a sort of a shared brotherhood of misery. Boston had the ball-through-Bill-Buckner's-legs debacle. Upstate New York had the Scott Norwood-far-right-field-goal miss. (Poor Ned had no idea the number of Championship Duck Boat Victory parades that awaited Boston sports. You can see why New York locals might get a bit, um, 'testy' over our Patriots bravado.)

We finished our meal and were headed out to the parking lot when Ned grunted, "Massholes" under his breath and stuck out a leg. Beef stumbled and dropped his plastic Diner bag of souvenirs. Kevin was never one to back down from a confrontation no matter how big the opponent, plus he always, *always* defended Boston sports teams, so when Beef went down Kevin immediately shot into action and got up and into Ned's grill.

Now let me tell you a bit more about this Ned guy. He was quite possibly the largest human being I'd ever seen. When he stood up, he had a monster frame. His thick matt of black hair was tucked under a John Deere hat and spilled down the sides of his face to a full black beard that covered his cheekbones and neck.

The whole Diner fell silent as Ned and Kevin eyed each other up and down (more *up* for Kevin) like two vicious dogs preparing to battle. I actually think they growled.

It could have gone either way until Beef bent for his souvenir bag and came between them.

"Sorry about that," he said, again trying to keep the peace. "I...I didn't see your leg there."

"Leave it alone Ned," Cheryl shouted from behind the counter, clearly the only one who could tame Ned the savage beast. We took that as our cue to get the hell out of the Diner and headed out into the car.

When we got there, Beef tossed the souvenir bag onto the back dash, adding to his already cluttered shopping spree, then unbuckled his pants and crawled across the back seat.

"I gotta lay down," he groaned.

"I told you not to eat so many cream puffs, you idiot," Kevin barked, still revved up from the confrontation with Ned.

"I know," Beef sighed. "Just let me lay down for a bit."

"You guys should really go gluten free," I told them. "It changed my life."

Joe grabbed the last cream puff out of Beef's hand and the three of us crammed into the front seat.

"Why don't you just get rid of these things," I said struggling to toss the huge 8-track case to the back.

"Careful with those tapes," Kevin yelled.

"You guys ever use that internet thing?" Beef piped up from the back. "I hear that's a good place to buy and sell stuff."

"Shut the fuck up back there," Kevin snapped. "And we're not sitting three across the whole way!"

That *'internet thing.'* Classic Beef. I'd forgotten about his stupid life observations and non sequiturs. Like the time he asked about a homeless guy's ability to make signs. 'I get how they can find cardboard, like, pizza boxes and beer cases and stuff. But where to do they find the black Magic Markers to write on them?' Or the time he argued that the weather forecaster on TV said wind*shield* factor instead of wind*chill* factor. Beef fought that argument for days. 'Yeah, they measure the temperature on a car windshield. Like, 'Careful out there today, people. The windshield factor is minus 10 degrees.'"

You gotta love that guy.

Kevin sat behind the wheel and fumbled with the keys. It took a few tries, but the Love Boat engine finally turned over. We drove out of the lot and pulled onto the road, when the music suddenly stopped and magnetic tape began to spit from the stereo.

"We got a bleeder!" Joe yelled.

"Aww, shit!" Kevin said, slamming the brakes.

This caused Joe to jolt forward and send the cream puff directly into his face.

They say timing is everything in life. Well, this was one of those times because when Joe bent to retrieve the cream puff, Ned and Chester pulled alongside us in their pickup truck. When they looked over, all they could see was me and Kevin, sitting *really* close, side by side in the front seat.

Oh, and I was applying lip balm in the rear-view mirror. See what I mean about timing?

It's amazing what you can hear through the crack of a partially opened window, because Ned and Chester heard the following exchange:

"Fix your pants," I yelled to Beef laying down across the back. "Joe's gonna come back there with you."

"Better leave room for Jimmy," Kevin added. "He's probably all stiff and hard by now."

And then, as if right on cue, Joe reappeared in the front seat. The side of his face was covered in cream filling. Ned's eyes grew wide as saucers and I'm pretty sure Chester began to dry heave.

Then it got worse.

While Kevin gathered up the runaway streaming tape from the broken 8-track, Joe opened the front door and hopped out to get in back. That's when good old Ned and Chester saw Beef laying across the seat --- with his pants unbuckled.

I laugh about it now, but it wasn't funny at the time. Turns out that in addition to being a deer hunter, a Bills fan, and bad dresser, Ned was blatantly homophobic.

How do I know this?

Because he was reaching for a shotgun mounted on his truck's cab behind him.

Suddenly, *thankfully,* lights flashed, and a siren blared. A cop car was behind us. Now, I'm not 100% positive, but I think pointing a loaded rifle out a car window is against the law, even in rural upstate New York.

All Ned could do was watch as we drove away.

And he was seething.

Not about the cops. Not about the Patriots jersey. Not even about us singing 'Dancing Queen' at the top of our lungs. Ned was staring at the plastic souvenir bag piled along the back dash.

Beef took the wrong one.

And Ned was going to get his back.

A hand slides an 8-track cassette into the car stereo.

Music blares from the speakers.

"Let the good times roll

Let them knock you around

Let the good times roll

Let them make you a clown"

-The Cars

CLEVELAND, OHIO

It was well past ten o'clock at night when we arrived at the funeral home that held Jimmy's body. Obviously, the place was closed. Not a lot of 24-hour funeral homes, even in Cleveland.

"So, what's the plan, Kev?" I asked. "We gonna hijack the hearse?"

"Plan? I don't have a *plan*, Hollywood," Kevin snapped back.

"Maybe you should have bought Mike's book," Joe remarked dripping with sarcasm, then did his best smarmy imitation of my infomercial. "*A FIVE POINT PLAN FOR SUCCESS. GIMME 5!*"

"You know, you might benefit from it," I started. "It could help you to harness some of that negative energy and..."

Kevin's eyes shot daggers.

I shut up.

Beef was visibly shaken as he looked at the Funeral Home. I guess the gravity of the situation was starting to sink in.

"Are we gonna have to see Jimmy?" he asked in a wobbly voice,

"No, Beef," Kevin reassured him like a father telling his son there are no monsters under the bed. "Jimmy's in a body bag for transportation."

"Good," Beef replied softly.

I turned to Joe. "You're a lawyer. Isn't this against the law or something?"

"Federal Tax Attorney," Joe replied as if the words 'Federal' and 'Tax' and 'Attorney' actually hurt as they came out of his mouth.

Kevin spoke up.

"As long as they have the body embalmed before it crosses state lines, the Funeral Director can assign a Transportation Agent. Could be anyone. Might as well be us."

"I don't even want to know how you know all that," Joe said from the back.

"It's not an original idea," Kevin said looking at Joe in the rear-view mirror. "Gram Parsons. 1973. Have Mike look it up in his stupid little computer phone there."

"It's called an iPhone," I said rolling my eyes. "It plays music too."

"Blow me," Kevin snapped back, then started to explain. "Gram Parsons was a guitarist for The Byrds. He OD'd at twenty-six. His family wanted him buried in New Orleans, but his buddies knew he wanted to be cremated and have his ashes spread at Joshua Tree. So, they grabbed a bunch of Jack Daniels, stole a hearse and drove out to LAX to get his body."

Joe shook his head and sighed, "I shoulda been a rock star."

"Pretty fuckin' bad ass, right?" Kevin added.

I read the rest aloud from my little 'computer phone.'

"Kevin's right. When they got to the desert, they poured gas all over the casket. Too much apparently, because the whole thing went up in a huge fireball. They were fined $750 for leaving the ashes."

"Seven hundred and fifty dollars!" Beef shouted. "I can't afford that. How much would that fine be now? What if we get caught? Jeeze."

"Take it easy, Beef. It's not like we're gonna torch Jimmy," I reassured him.

Beef was visibly upset.

"I...I don't think I can do this, guys."

"You know what?" Joe said, then imitated a line from Steve Martin's comedy album. "We need to get *smaaaaall.*"

"Anyone bring weed?" Kevin asked.

"Sure, I got some. Oh, where did I leave it?" I said patting myself down. "I know. In 1981! Jesus, guys, come on!"

"Bet I know where we could find some," Kevin said with a confident smirk.

Joe looked at his watch and grumbled.

"We'll never make it."

DORCHESTER, MA

While the four of us went on a late-night search for weed, Detective Richie Kelly was back in Boston pouring over the McShane case. At ten o'clock at night, most people his age are watching the news or getting ready for bed.

Not Kelly.

He rarely got more than three or four hours of sleep a night. I'm sure it had something to do with all that Dunkin' Donuts coffee, but Richie Kelly wasn't about to give up his six-cup-a-day habit.

Something about the McShane case nagged at him. Every cop south of Boston knew the McShane's record and every person from the neighborhood knew their criminal reputation. With other crimes, there would be press conferences on street corners and the story would lead the ten o'clock news. Not Old Man McShane's death. No one really gave a shit that another Whitey Bulger wanna-be scumbag was taken out.

Seamus McShane came to Boston from Ireland in the early 1960's. As a young man, he worked odd jobs around Brighton and Allston. A day laborer on home improvement crews. A bartender. Trash pick-up around the MDC rinks. In each job, Seamus always found a way to pocket a little something for himself. It was just the way he was built.

In 1974 McShane did time in Walpole prison for selling cocaine. When he got out, he had made all the right connections to help distribute on the streets of Dorchester.

A talent he handed down to his redheaded boys.

Ronan and Corey in turn built a nice business of loan sharking and drug dealing. Otherwise known to them as 'Finance and Pharmaceuticals.' Two words I doubt they could even spell.

Richie Kelly sat at the small Formica kitchen table of his one-bedroom apartment. The whole place had the look of a man who spent years living alone. Dishes piled in the sink. A single worn leather chair in the center of the room surrounded by old copies of the Boston Herald.

Of course, Kelly was a Herald man. He hated the liberal slant of the Boston Globe. In his opinion, anyone who read the Globe was in the 'Yankees/Stones/Starbucks' camp.

He sat staring at the police crime scene photos of Seamus McShane's bloodied and beaten body as it lay in the abandoned Navy shipyard. For generations, shipbuilding was the way of life for thousands in Quincy, Dorchester, and Weymouth. But in the spring of 1986, General Dynamics shut down for good. The whole area had become a forgotten strip of no man's land. And the perfect place to dispose a body.

Kim Bletzer was right about a couple things; Richie Kelly did have the highest solve rate in the unit, and McShane's murder wasn't random.

He poured himself another cup of coffee and thought on it some more, staring out the window at the city as though the correct answer were out there somewhere.

A hand slides an 8-track cassette into the car stereo.

Music blares from the speakers.

"Well I remember every little thing
as if it happened only yesterday.
Parking by the lake and there was
not another car in sight"

-Meat Loaf

CLEVELAND, OHIO

Kevin picked the lock to Jimmy's apartment with the same effortless confidence he displayed on the football fields. Typical Kevin, making it look easy when in fact it's hard. And in this case illegal. Nothing ever stood in his way. I wondered what it must be like to be a guy like Kevin, so confident and utterly fearless. I, on the other hand, was a complete nervous wreck.

"Perfect," I grumbled looking up and down the dark hallway. "Wait till US Magazine gets a hold of this."

Joe mocked me. *"Stars. They're just like us. They break into dead friends' apartments to steal pot!"*

"Shut the fuck up, will ya?" Kevin loudly Irish-whispered, then opened the door.

We wandered in, deeply unsettled.

No one said anything, we just looked around at the small sadly under-furnished apartment that was Jimmy's time capsule. Carlton Fisk posters hung on the wall alongside Elvis Costello. Cape Cod souvenirs lined a shelf. Sand crusted beer caps lay at the bottom of an empty fish tank. A single mattress and box spring were placed on the floor with a small transistor radio on the bedside table.

There was no television because Jimmy loved to read. I remember that we used to make fun of him for it. I mean, who reads in the summer when school is out? Jimmy did. He devoured books. Especially European history about Scandinavian folklore. He obviously still loved that stuff because Beef found a half-finished plastic model of a Viking ship that Jimmy had been working on.

Joe called to us from across the room.

"You guys remember this?"

He was pointing to the black guitar case that used to hold his prized Carlton Fisk baseball bat. Kevin hustled over and grabbed the case. He eagerly tossed it onto the mattress and snapped the silver buckles open.

His face fell.

The case was empty, except for a black and white photograph wedged into the back of the red velvet. Young Jimmy and Mr. Callahan at the beach.

Our beach.

Lewis Bay.

A quiet sadness circled the room.

"I guess Lake Eire is sorta like Cape Cod Bay," Beef said looking out the window to the shimmering waters in the distance.

"Jimmy sure loved the Cape," Joe said softly.

"The Jimmy we knew left a long time ago," Kevin said slowly closing the empty guitar case.

I was on the other side of the room flipping through a box of old record albums that I found in the corner. Each one was a memory of a better time.

Frampton Comes Alive. Born to Run. The Stranger.

Jesus, this stuff was awesome. Take away the 'toot toot beep beep' Disco shit, and we really grew up with some great music.

There was something at the bottom of the box, hidden in the back behind The Rolling Stones *Exile on Main Street*. I knew what it was immediately, and quickly put it in my pocket before anyone noticed.

I didn't say anything to the guys about my discovery. I turned to them, my tone firm and direct, and said, "We've seen enough. Let's get outta here."

Kevin agreed. It was just too creepy being in Jimmy's empty apartment.

"What about the weed?" Joe asked.

We all knew where to look next.

ROCK AND ROLL HALL OF FAME -

"You coming?" Beef asked as we all exited the car. Well, everyone except Kevin. He sat behind the wheel with a scowl on his face.

"I refuse to go in there," he replied like a stubborn child "Not until they induct Gram Parsons and the Flying Burrito Brothers."

He wasn't budging, so the rest of us took off.

The Security Guard that night and every night for the past 15 years since the Rock and Roll Hall of Fame opened was Lenny Palmer. Lenny was a leftover from Opening Day in 1986 when someone in the Marketing Department had the idea to hire people who resembled Rock Stars. Back in the day, Lenny resembled '80's rocker Billy Idol.

Unfortunately, age and too many Mid-Western all-you-can-eat buffets have taken a toll on Lenny. He now resembled a pot-bellied, lip-snarling Meat Loaf (the singer, Michael Lee Aday, known professionally as Meat Loaf, not the dinner meal).

Lenny sat at the front desk reading a Rolling Stone Magazine, angrily drawing mustaches on the photos of current rock stars. Apparently, Lenny had a huge chip on his shoulder since both of his doppelgängers, young Billy Idol, and now heavy-set middle-aged Meat Loaf, have yet to be inducted into the Rock and Roll Hall of Fame.

I approached the entrance with my best smarmy-LA-Motivational-Speaker-Guy mode and laid it on thick.

"Good evening, sir."

"We're closed," Lenny grunted, his eyes never leaving the magazine.

"And how are we...

"We're closed."

"...on this fine Cleveland evening?"

"We're closed."

Billy Idol and Meat Loaf may not make it into the Rock and Roll Hall of Fame, but Lenny Palmer was certainly doing his best to get into the Security Guard Hall of Fame.

"Um, we're with the Make-a-Wish Foundation. Scandinavian Branch," I said, then pointed to Beef. "This is Sven."

Joe joined in. He leaned towards Lenny and whispered, "He doesn't have much time."

"We're closed," was all Lenny said, again.

"We just arrived in your lovely city," I continued.

"From Sweden," Joe piped in.

"Yes, well, we, ah…we heard ABBA was inducted?" I asked.

Lenny groaned. Clearly, he was not an ABBA fan.

I put an arm around Beef.

"Sven here is probably the world's largest, ah, I mean *biggest* ABBA fan."

Joe added, "His last wish is to see the ABBA exhibit in all its ABBA-dabba-de-liciousness."

Lenny finally raised his eyes and looked directly at Sven...I mean Beef.

"Uh, huh. What's your favorite ABBA song?" he asked.

Beef was caught off guard.

"Favorite? Oh gosh, there are so many," he replied.

"Name one. Just one," Lenny quizzed him.

"Just one, huh?" Beef asked, totally flustered. Joe and I could literally see the pores open on Beef's skin and the sweat beginning to pool.

"Boy, let's see," Beef went on, trying his best. "There's so many. Um. There's the one about the girl. The Mom. The Momma! The Dancing Momma? Jeeze..."

Beef was a mess.

"Oh shit, here we go," Joe said as he watched the sweat start to run down Beef's face. "Better get a towel and head for higher ground!"

Beef punched Joe on the arm, then gave it another try.

"The Queen. Something with a Queen in it, right?"

After a moment of trying to remember another ABBA song, Beef just gave up and blurted, "You know what? ABBA sucks!"

"You know what? You suck at talking," I scolded him.

"No, he's right. ABBA does suck," Lenny replied, finally breaking his 'tough-guy Security Guard character' and making eye contact. "First truthful thing you boys have said all night. What the hell ABBA is doing in this sacred place is beyond me. I mean, come on!"

"So, you'll let us in?" Beef asked excitedly.

"No. We're closed," Lenny snapped yet again.

"Yeah, we kinda got that," Joe remarked.

Lenny may not have been friendly, but he was consistent.

"Get going before I have you all arrested for trespassing," he said then turned his attention back to defacing Rock Star's pictures in the magazine.

Then, as if a lightbulb went on in his head, Lenny looked up at me.

"Wait a second. You're that guy on TV."

Joe put an arm around my shoulder and mocked, "That's him alright. *Gimme 5!*"

A small smile finally wrinkled Lenny's face.

"You must be Jimmy Callahan's friends. He talked about you guys all the time,"

"He did?" Beef asked.

"Yeah. Which one of you went to church in Hyannis wearing a Dead Kennedys T-Shirt?"

Me and Beef immediately pointed at Joe.

"And you shook Rose Kennedy's hand?" Lenny laughed.

Joe got all defensive. "I forgot I had it on! It was the Sign of Peace for cryin' out loud. What was I supposed to do?"

"Real shame about Jimmy," Lenny admitted, then he looked us up and down, head to toe. "He hated ABBA you know."

"Oh...we know," we all agreed.

I looked Lenny in the eye, almost pleading.

"We came to collect some of Jimmy's things. For the funeral."

That seemed to resonate because Lenny looked around the empty parking lot and then said, "You got 10 minutes."

"Don't worry," Joe said to him with a wink. "We'll make like a bat outta hell."

****

Kevin sat under the dim hue of a parking light, the night's hush falling over the area as he looked across the still waters of Lake Erie to FirstEnergy Stadium, home of the Cleveland Browns. It was a symbolic nod to what might have been. A football career and a dream over before it could even start.

He flipped the car visor down above his head and a thick Polaroid fell to his lap. **Junior Prom 1979** was written in black ink along the white border. A young couple stared back at him; teenage Kevin in a powder blue tuxedo beside Katie in a matching Gunny Sack dress.

Kevin stared deeply at the photo in his hand. He wants to tell the teenager in the picture so many things. Be smart. Cherish it. Embrace it. Love it. Because that moment right there? That's as good as it gets. Don't fuck it up, kid.

But it's too late for that. E   motions began to well up inside him like a balloon until Kevin couldn't hold it in anymore.

And he began to cry.

Slowly at first, then sobs, his whole-body convulsing in sadness.

****

As soon as we made our way into the Rock and Roll Hall of Fame, Joe wandered off, bug-eyed, like a kid's first visit to Disney World.

Beef and I were on a mission and made a beeline for the maintenance room. We found the locker marked CALLAHAN and opened it to Jimmy's final view. Taped to the inside of the locker door was a 'Greetings from Cape Cod' postcard. Below the postcard, Jimmy had scrawled lyrics in thick black ink.

'Is there only pain and hatred and misery?'

"Elvis Costello," Beef said sadly. "Jimmy's favorite."

We stood in silence for a moment, the weight of it sinking in.

I knew good old Lenny Palmer wasn't going to let us wander the hallowed floors of the Rock and Roll Hall of Fame for long. We had a job to do. I reached my hand deep into the top locker and *"Bingo!"* I slowly pulled out small, clear baggie of weed.

"Where the hell is Joe?" I said, anxious to leave.

"Can you go look for him?" Beef asked softly. I could tell he was upset. "I'm just gonna sit here a minute if that's okay."

"Sure, sure," I said. "I knew Jimmy wouldn't let us down."

As soon as I was gone, Beef leaned forward, reached for something hidden in the back of the locker and whispered, "I knew Jimmy wouldn't let me down either."

Suddenly, alarms went off. Buzzing. Screaming. Braying. The place was blinding with flashing lights. Beef came limping out of the maintenance room to see Joe racing towards him.

"What happened?" Beef yelled.

"Just run," Joe screamed as he ran past us. "Run!"

I swear I could hear the ABBA song 'Waterloo' playing in the background as we broke into a thunderous run. Lenny Palmer our friendly Security Guard was now mad as, well, mad as a 'bat outta hell' (see what I did there?) and chasing after us. It was absolute mayhem. All of us running and sweating, our legs shaking with nerves, our hearts pounding as we slid past exhibits, knocked into guitars, crashed into drum sets.

Finally, through some miracle, we found an emergency exit door. I was about to lay my hand on the handle when Beef stopped me. "Wait! This says 'Emergency Exit' only. The alarm will go... oh, right."

Classic Beef.

We bolted out the door.

"Where the hell is Kevin?!" I shouted breathlessly looking out into the empty parking lot.

Just then, tires screamed, and the Love Boat came flying. Kevin screeched on the brakes and we hopped in just before Lenny reached us.

As we peeled out into the night, Beef hung out the window, pumped his arms, and screamed back at Lenny, "Rock and....Agh...!"

He didn't finish.

He swallowed a bug.

SULLIVAN AUTO REPAIR – DORCHESTER, MA

Billy was working late at the garage when the McShane brothers wandered in.

"Where's yer old man at, yo?" Corey yelled out.

Ronan glared at his ridiculous 'Gansta' brother, seething at his Ghetto-American vernacular.

"He's not here. Should be back tomorrow," Billy told them, completely unaware of the danger he was in.

Ronan fired up a cigarette.

"You, ah, you can't smoke in here," Billy said.

Ronan ignored the comment, took a long pull on the cigarette and began to walk around the garage.

"Left ya alone here, did he? Petrol. Oily rags. Place is a real fire hazard. Shame if something was to happen to it." He stopped and looked directly at the teenager. "Or you."

The hairs on the back of Billy's neck stood up.

Ronan pointed to Beef's minivan. "That the Deli man's car, is it?"

Beef changed the oil in his car every three thousand miles like clockwork. Kevin gave him free service and Beef gave him free Italian subs. A fair exchange, I guess.

Corey slid into the minivan and began to fiddle under the dashboard.

"Can..can I help you there?" Billy asked, feeling uneasy as he motioned towards Beef's car. But Ronan blocked his path and his view.

"Don't mind him. Me brother think's he may have left something in there. You, ah, you didn't happen to see a bat around did ye?"

"A bat?" Billy asked, his face slanted with confusion.

Ronan smiled his sinister psychotic smile. "We're old friends of your Da, lad. We used to play ball with them when we was kids. We're lookin' for a wooden baseball bat."

Billy just shrugged like a confused teenager.

"Why don't you call him on the mobile and let him know the McShanes boys stopped by," Ronan told him.

"Cell phone? My Dad?" Billy replied. "You must not know him that well. He hasn't bought anything new in years."

Corey climbed out of the minivan and gave his brother an 'all set' nod.

Ronan turned to Billy, dropped the lit cigarette to the ground at his feet and gave the boy a heavy, menacing tap on the cheek.

"Tell your father we'll be waiting."

Across the street, Detective Richie Kelly sat in an unmarked Crown Victoria, his cigar glowing in the dark. He took a long puff and peered through the flume of smoke, watching as the McShane brothers left the garage.

A hand slides an 8-track cassette into the car stereo.

Music blares from the speakers.

*"Hello old friend,
It's really good to see you once again."*

-Eric Clapton

CLEVELAND, OHIO

We talked about grabbing a hotel room, but since our Steve McQueen-like Great Escape from the Rock and Roll Hall of Fame we thought it was best to keep a low profile. It was only a few hours till the Funeral Home opened, so we decided to gut it out, park across the street in the lot of a 24-hour convenience store and sleep in the Love Boat.

Just like old times. Like high school.

Most of the guys slept heavily through the night. I kept waking, especially since Beef snored like a buzz saw. Snoring and sweating. God, his wife Jeannie is an absolute saint. One of those people who is going to heaven straight through the turnstile.

I don't know what time it was, maybe 5:30 or 6:00 AM, but the sound of the car door woke me when Beef got out to use the bathroom inside the Convenience store. I rubbed my eyes and squinted as the rising sun bounced off the landscape and began to flood the car with the first light of day.

There's something fascinating about a sunrise. A new day. A new beginning. When Katie and I first moved to the west coast, we made a point to catch a sunrise together at least once a week. It always amazed me, the way the colors would come out of nowhere and surprise you.

I sat there and for the life of me couldn't remember the last time Katie and I watched the sunrise together.

I couldn't remember the last time Katie and I did *anything* together.

I'd never been to Cleveland. I never had any reason to go there. But I have to tell you, the sunrise on this morning for some reason was spectacular.

I didn't realize it, but Kevin was awake too, staring at the same rising sun. I don't know how long we both sat there watching the purples and pinks rise and steal into the sky. For a while, we sat in silence. He didn't know what I was thinking about, and I didn't know what he was thinking about either. But it didn't matter. We both just respected the quiet and each other's space, as if both of us silently knew if we had spoken it would ruin the moment.

And then I realized something - that's the thing about old friends. You don't *have* to say anything. It's already known what goes unsaid.

It's just that comfortable.

For me that was the best part of the trip. The most meaningful and the most real. That moment was mine. No editors. No Hollywood bullshit. No fans. No 'smarmy Mike' having to put on a show. There was nothing fake about any of it.

Just two old friends enjoying a quiet moment.

"We had some great times in this car," Kevin said finally breaking the silence.

"We sure did."

"Remember the night we snuck into the Braintree Drive-In and I wouldn't open the trunk?" he said with a smile. "I thought Beef was gonna piss his pants."

"He did."

"No," Kevin exclaimed.

"Yep. Beef said it was just sweat. But I could smell it."

Kevin laughed.

"God, Katie was so pissed," he reminisced. "She kept punching my arm, yelling at me to let you guys out."

We both smiled at the memory. There sure was something innocent and fun to those days. I turned to face him.

"Listen, Kev, about me and Kate. I need to tell you something."

But I never finished.

Beef came bouncing back into the car, giddy as an eight-year-old on Christmas morning. He was dressed head to toe in tacky Cleveland tourist clothes. A neon visor. A Rock and Roll Hall of Fame T-Shirt. An *I Heart Ohio* fanny pack.

He looked ridiculous.

"Jeannie and the kids are gonna love this stuff!" he said tossing yet another bag of souvenirs onto the crowded rear dash.

Joe woke up and looked at his watch.

"We're never gonna make it," he grumbled.

We waited and watched outside the funeral home, not sure exactly what the hell we were going to do next.

GET YOUR BARN RAISED AT THE FUZZY BUGGY

It was mid-morning, maybe 9:00 AM, by the time the funeral home opened. We were all a bit groggy after getting only a few hours of sleep, when suddenly a long black vehicle pulled out from behind the building.

Beef threw on a pair of oversized souvenir sunglasses he bought from the convenience store and said, "Cut the cake." (I swear we must have seen Animal House twenty times when it came out).

We drove for a while, staying a few car lengths back until we crossed into Pennsylvania. At this point, we were just happy to get out of Ohio, and I was glad that the car was headed east towards Boston.

"So, what do we do now, Kev?" I asked.

"I don't know. I'm kinda making this shit up as I go," he replied.

"Really?" Joe piped in. "You'd never know it. Things are going so well."

"He's gonna stop for food, right?" Beef said anxiously. "*We're* gonna stop for food, right?"

"I'm sure he'll stop for gas," Kevin said.

"Or gash," Joe replied pointing to a huge sign above the road.

THE FUZZY BUGGY

TUESDAY NIGHT BUD LITE MENNONITE NIGHT.

Now, this next part of the trip I'm not exactly sure how to explain. To be honest, I'm not even sure that it ever really happened. It's been a few years, and like any of our stories, it got bigger, we were drunker, thinner, the girls were hotter, and we all got laid. You know, it's kind of a guy thing. Stories sort of take on grand proportions over time. Joe used to say, 'Never let the truth stand in the way of a good story.'

So, this is what happened next.

We thought it was odd when the hearse left the highway. The driver had been going along at a pretty good clip, then for some strange reason he took an exit and drove along some long, windy back road.

We realized why once we followed him inside.

The Fuzzy Buggy was a cavernous barn that had been converted into some kind of weird bar/strip joint. Scantily clad Milk Maids wandered the room dressed in bonnets and aprons and pretty much nothing else. The place was surprisingly active for a mid-morning crowd. A bearded man dressed in a black straight-cut suit, suspenders, and a straw broad-brimmed hat stood perched in what I think was the DJ Booth/hay loft and announced, "That was Rebecca doing her interpretive dance to the movie 'Witness.' Please welcome Hester to the main stage."

"Is this place for real?" Beef asked with childlike innocence.

"Real Amish, fake tits," Joe said.

"Fake Amish, real tits. Who gives a shit, they got beer," Kevin said and made his way to the bar.

I was terrified of being recognized, so I grabbed Beef's oversized souvenir sunglasses. Joe turned to me and said, "You should be okay, Mike. I don't think this is your demographic."

"I hope the pole isn't made outta wood," Beef observed, his eyes glued to the dancer. "That's a tough area to get a splinter."

Joe shouted towards the stage, "Show us your buttons!" then took off with Beef to explore the place.

I was forced to join Kevin at the bar.

We stood there for a few moments in awkward silence, not knowing what to say to each other until we were finally greeted by a stone-faced Amish bartender. We were both quietly grateful for someone who kept us from having to recognize the strangers we had become.

"Bud. Bottle," Kevin told him.

They both glared at me awaiting my order as I scanned the bar.

"Hmmm...I'd love a martini," I said, being my typical pain in the ass. "What kind of vodka do you have? Stoli? Grey Goose? Belvedere?"

"Potato," the bartender replied flatly. Then he turned and poured clear liquid into a Mason jar and slid the glass in front of me.

"Can I at least get this shaken?" I asked, a bit put off.

Without missing a beat, the stoic bartender placed his enormous hand over the top of my drink and gave it a perfunctory shake. Then he plopped a radish into the glass and walked away.

Kevin shook his head.

"Do you automatically become a dick once you land in LA, or do they make you take a class?"

I ignored the comment and scanned the barn for Beef and Joe. "Where the hell did those two take off to?"

"I have no idea. Beef is probably looking for more souvenirs," Kevin said, leaning his elbows on the bar. "We were all supposed to take that road trip after college, remember?"

"We were? I don't remember that," I said.

"Yeah. I know. You seem to not remember a lot of things," Kevin replied with a bit of a sting.

I wasn't sure what he meant.

"You left to work on the Dukakis campaign," Kevin continued. "Then Carter, Kennedy, Mondale. 0 for 4 there, big guy. Might as well become a fuckin' Republican."

I gave a resigned smile and took another sip of my Mason jar potato martini. (It wasn't half bad!)

"Politics wasn't my game," I said. "But it was a great way to pick up girls. They were always so sad at the concession speeches."

Kevin just shook his head. He didn't have any patience for my flirtatious ways back in high school, and he certainly didn't approve of them now.

I took another sip.

"At least I was able to figure a way to spin that political bullshit into celebrity self-help bullshit. That's how I came up the Five Point Plan. *GIMME 5!*" I said and tried to give him a high-five.

Kevin ignored it and left me hanging.

"You still don't get it, do you?" he said coldly and took a long pull of his beer.

Our relationship was always strained. Growing up, I envied Kevin and feared him and sometimes, I'll admit it, I hated him. He had it all. Looks. Athlete. Car. Most of all, he had Katie. We were friends back in the day. But now? Now it felt like we were two middle-aged strangers in some weird converted barn/bar/strip joint just politely sizing each other up.

"I get it Kev. I should have stayed in touch more," I finally admitted. "I'm here now, aren't I?"

Kevin stared straight ahead.

"You're here because you thought it was the right thing to do, not because you wanted to."

"You're wrong," I shot back. "I came back for me. I thought, maybe coming home might help."

I lowered my head and checked my cellphone (again) to see if anyone (Katie) had called me. (She hadn't).

"Will you leave that Goddamn thing alone for a minute? You're worse than my kid for Chrissake. *You're* the people who are obsessed, not me!" Kevin snapped.

"You mean like your Bonneville and the alphabetized 8-tracks?" I replied.

That one stung.

Kevin paused before answering. He knew I was right. Maybe it was the mid-morning beer, or the setting, or the whole road trip situation, but after a brief moment of reflection, Kevin began to pick at the label of his Budweiser bottle.

"Those 8-tracks are about the closest I've ever come to a commitment. There's a whole world in that case. It takes me places - better places than the one I live in, that's for sure. Those tapes. The car. They just remind me of better times. I never wanted it to end."

He paused for a moment.

"I'm really good at the past. It's the present I have problems with. That stuff kinda helps me from floating away, ya know? It's not the tapes...it's just, it's…"

He was struggling to capture the right words, then finally said, "It's just something to hold on to."

We both let that lie on the bar for a bit.

"You do realize this is crazy, us bringing Jimmy home, right?" I said, then turned to him with a smirk. "But it's been *wicked pissah so fah*."

"Woah! Did I just hear a little Dorchester creep back there, kid?" Kevin said full of mock surprise. "Better be careful, you don't want the Paparazzi to hear you."

We smiled together.

Finally.

"I know this whole idea is stupid. Probably even illegal. No, *definitely* illegal. But people do stupid things every day. Believe me, I've done my share," Kevin said turning his eyes away. "But most of them are meaningless stupid things. I figured, why not do *one* thing that mattered."

He held the beer to his lips then said, "at least to me it would."

I sort of felt bad for him. He wasn't the broad-shouldered linebacker who roamed the middle of the field wreaking havoc on tailbacks and fullbacks who dared to enter his lane. Kevin almost seemed mortal. Tired. Weakened.

I looked him in the eye because it was important.

"It matters to Jimmy," I said.

And for a moment we both saw the thing that made us friends.

"Just wish all this was for a different reason, ya know?" he replied.

"You couldn't protect him forever, Kev."

"Shit he went through? That kid was tougher than all of us. He didn't need me. I just never had the balls to…"

His voice trailed off.

"To what?" I asked.

But Kevin never did finish that thought. He just drained his beer in one long pull.

"When the hell did we get old?" he asked as the Amish bartender brought another round.

"I know, right? Get your prostate checked yet?" I asked, lifting two fingers in the air and doing my best swipe-the-Vaseline-and-get-the-fingers-ready-to-probe motion.

Kevin held up four fingers.

I was confused. Four?

"Four feet of fiber optic cable, my man," he said. "Colonoscopy last year. Had a bit of a scare."

The news took me back.

"I'm sorry, Kev. I…I didn't know," I said and immediately knew how stupid that sounded.

Of course I didn't know. How could I have? I never called. I hadn't been back to Boston in years. I get Christmas cards from Beef and Jeannie every year showing off their husky kids. Joe sends an email every now and then with something that he thinks is funny. But I hardly ever email back or reach out to the guys and ask things like 'How's Kevin's colon?' or anything like that.

"You okay?"

"Clean as a whistle inside and out," he said, but I could tell it rattled him. He looked old to me. I felt old too.

We stood there staring at our drinks.

"It's good to see you, man," I finally said. And I really meant it.

Kevin raised his Bud bottle.

"To assholes."

"To assholes," I responded.

We clinked glasses, Mason jar to Bud bottle.

****

Meanwhile, at the other end of the barn, Joe was busy talking to a couple of Milk Maids, Rebecca and Hester.

Joe never married, he was always too focused on his job, or, as Kevin would remind him, he was always too busy sticking his head up his father's ass.

Joe's father was a pretty big deal in Massachusetts politics, and he rode that leverage all the way to Washington DC. It was a career journey he expected his only son to follow. Girlfriends, wives and family would have to wait.

"Interesting place you got here," Joe said to the girls.

"It beats selling roadside souvenirs," Rebecca replied curtly.

"Yep. We're just livin' the dream," Hester added looking sad and bored.

Joe looked around the barn, intrigued. "How do you keep track of all the cash? No receipts. Must be very confusing, tax-wise."

"Not really," Hester replied. "The Elders have us set up as a 501c3 non-profit."

Joe's Tax Attorney ears perked up.

Hester continued.

"Under Section 511, an organization is not subject to tax on its unrelated business income..."

Joe added, "...whether or not the organization actually makes a profit..."

They finished together. "...but not including selling donated merchandise."

Joe gazed into her eyes and said, "I think I'm in love."

Rebecca broke their trance.

"Plus, Ezekial runs Bingo in here every other Sabbath. Keeps us clean from any prying Government assholes."

"You know, I wanted to be a rock star?" Joe admitted. "Drink shitloads of Jack Daniels. Smash guitars. Throw TV's out hotel windows. But my father wanted me to be a tax attorney. Pretty exciting, right?"

"Daddy issues, huh?" Rebecca shrugged. "Grab a pole and get in line."

Joe thought for a moment, then exclaimed, "Assholes. You're right. I'm just gonna be another prying Government asshole. An asshole looking for loopholes. You know what I mean?"

Rebecca's face contorted with confusion.

"Loopholes? Oh, we're not allowed to have buttons."

Hester chimed in.

"My mother has my whole life planned out. Wants me to sell quilts to the tourists. Just like her. And her mother. And everyone else in my family."

Joe recognized her pain, and suddenly there was a real spark between them. That's when he saw the hearse driver heading off with a Milk Maid to The Cider Room.

"Looks like Jimmy's not the only one gonna be stiff for the ride home," he said aloud. "Could you girls give me a hand with something?"

And then Joe devised a plan.

A hand slides an 8-track into the car stereo.

Music blares from the speakers.

'Don't cry

Don't raise your eye

It's only teenage wasteland'

-The Who

SULLIVAN AUTO REPAIR - DORCHESTER, MA

Billy and Kevin were close when Billy was young. They used to go to Red Sox games together and sit in the bleachers. Kevin taught Billy how to throw a slow looping curve with a wiffleball. They even spent time listening to music together. *Kevin's* music, not the radio Top 40.

But then the call would come from Mrs. Callahan. 'Jimmy didn't come home last night.' 'Could you please come over. Jimmy is 'sick' again,' and Kevin would take off. Sometimes right in the middle of an inning, or a pitch, or a song.

At first it didn't bother him. Billy was young and he just shrugged it off. He got used to his father choosing Jimmy over him. But once Billy became a teenager…well, it started to hurt. And instead of saying anything, Billy just decided to shut down. At about thirteen Billy stopped trying to have any kind of relationship with his distant father.

Kevin could sense the change. He tried to get their relationship back on track, but it was too far gone. He learned to asked open-ended questions to try to get a real conversation going. 'How's school going' or 'How was practice,' but the sullen teenager never really engaged. It was no use. Billy still answered with a 'yes' a 'no' or nothing at all. Most subjects between them just fizzled out after two or three awkward exchanges.

It was breaking Kevin's heart.

But what Kevin didn't know was that Billy's heart was already broken.

And had been for a while.

Anger and sadness have a way of settling in and taking root in a person. Eventually it gets so you can't tell the two apart, and you end up just trying to live your life, all the while dying in increments. That seemed to be a pattern with the Sullivan men.

Maybe Billy just reminded Kevin too much of the mistakes he'd made.

Billy sat alone in the garage, like he did every Saturday, knowing his father was off somewhere helping Jimmy. Again.

The bright light of day streamed in as a well-dressed man in his mid-fifties entered the garage with a folded newspaper under his arm.

"Excuse me," he called out to Billy. "I'm here about the car."

"Sure, which one?" Billy said, doing his best to act like he was in charge.

"The Bonneville."

"We aren't working on a Bonneville," Billy replied.

The man handed Billy his copy of the Boston Globe.

"The '74 Bonneville. The one listed here in the paper. I spoke with a Mr. Sullivan. He didn't sell it already, did he?"

Billy was totally confused.

"No. What?"

"Could you have him call me?" the man said as he wrote down his number.

Billy stared at the ad in the Globe. It was all right there in black and white. 1974 Bonneville. Mint condition. Only sixty-two thousand miles.

His head was spinning. Why would his father sell his beloved car? His *grandfather's* beloved car. It's 'The Love Machine' for crying out loud.

It really is amazing what teenagers don't see.

They're so busy being teenagers that they never see the bills mounting up in a small wicker basket beside the refrigerator. Or the laundry piled up high by the machine. Or the early morning coffee brewing as a parent gets up at dawn to put in an extra shift just so they can buy their kid a new glove or pair of skates. It's not that kids don't care, it's just that they never notice all that grown-up stuff.

They never see the worry, or the stress, or even, sometimes, the love.

Billy was particularly oblivious to his father's life. If he *had* paid attention, even a little bit, he might have seen the Holy Cross tuition statement sitting on top of his father's desk with the words 'First Semester Payment' circled in red. He might have seen the Bank of America letter that showed a low balance alert. If Billy paid attention more, he might even know that for the past year an envelope containing a few hundred dollars left Sullivan's Garage every month, addressed to Mrs. Callahan.

But Billy is a typical teenager and he never paid attention to any of that 'grown-up' stuff. He didn't see the tuition bills, or the bank statements, or the envelopes.

And Billy most certainly didn't see the duct taped package Corey McShane hid under the dashboard of Beef's minivan.

The wires flowed to the ignition.

FUZZY BUGGY

Joe bolted towards me and Kevin in the parking lot dangling a set of keys in his hand.

"For a gal who grew up without buttons, she sure is dexterous," he said.

Thanks to Rebecca and Hester's nimble handywork on the hearse driver while he was, um, 'distracted' in The Cider Room, we were able to open the back door of the hearse.

We stared at the casket.

There was a brief moment of silence while we all looked at each other, unsure of what to do next, of what to think of or even consider. A look of desperate sadness passed over our faces. More than sadness, it was realization. The realization that our friend Jimmy was inside. The Jimmy that we played wiffleball with. The Jimmy who loved music, especially Elvis Costello. The Jimmy who was really into Vikings and reading and history. The Jimmy who was smarter than all of us without even trying.

Our friend Jimmy was dead.

Jesus Christ, Jimmy Callahan was dead.

This was all real now. Scary real.

"Well," I said looking at Kevin seeking our next move. "This was your idea."

"I know, but..." Kevin said, looking too shook up to make a decision.

Joe could sense our reluctance, so he jumped in.

"Listen to me. I sit in an office all day daydreaming about our high school days. It's fucking depressing. This road trip is officially the coolest thing I've done in, like, twenty years."

Joe was a man possessed. He had lived his whole life cautiously, on someone else's terms and maneuvers and motivations. This was his time. He looked at us and in his best Elwood Blues Brothers manner said, "It's 500 miles to Boston, we got a full tank of gas, half a bag of weed, and we have dark souvenir glasses."

Kevin snapped out of it and stared at us with a look that was both confident and scary. It was the look of a linebacker who somehow knew the exact play that was being called.

All he said was, "Hit it."

We had a job to do.

We opened the casket, grabbed the thick plastic body bag, and carried it from the hearse to the Love Boat.

"We really should tell General Motors about this cooler/trunk/mobile morgue idea," Joe said as we laid the bag into the oversized trunk.

"You two go find Beef before the driver gets back here," I told them. "I gotta call Katie."

It was almost the truth.

As soon as they took off, I began to press numbers on my cell phone.

I had a plan of my own.

****

Let me try and explain 'The Cider Room.' I'm guessing this is the Amish version of what high class patrons of a gentlemen's club might refer to as 'The Champagne Room.' It's usually a VIP area where a customer can purchase some 'exclusive' time with one of the, um, entertainers.

In this particular establishment, The Cider Room was a roped off corner of the barn. Customers sat on bales of hay behind swinging saloon doors as Milk Maids gave private dances. A neon sign above the rooms read 'Churn Baby Churn.'

Kevin and Joe went in search of our missing friend Beef. As soon as they entered the 'VIP' area, they heard voices from behind one of the swinging doors:

"Wow."

"It's so big."

"I don't think I've ever seen anything like it. It's enormous!"

Suddenly, they heard Beef's voice.

"Thanks. I call it 'The 10-inch Beef Special.'"

Joe and Kevin looked at each other. Shocked. Horrified. Disgusted. Fearing the worst, they burst through the swinging doors screaming, "No, Beef! Stop!"

There was our man-child friend Beef surrounded by adoring Milk Maids. It was almost like a beautiful Hallmark moment.

Almost.

To their relief, Beef was proudly showing off photos of his deli sandwiches. The floor around him was littered with Amish knick-knacks. Beef had hit the souvenir motherlode. Mason jars of preserves. Quilts for Jeannie. Straw hats for the kids. A 'Barn Raising for Dummies' book.

"Careful girls," Joe told them. "He has a gland problem."

Beef looked up, oblivious as ever.

"Hey guys. What's up?"

They grabbed Beef and rushed out.

****

I had just finished making my call in the parking lot. It was important and I didn't need the guys around to hear it. Satisfied, I hung up and was about to go looking for those knuckleheads, when a huge hand fell on my shoulder, spun me around and grabbed me by the throat.

"Whatchu doin' here, pretty boy?" a voice boomed. "This place is for men who like women."

It was Ned, all six foot five of him, glaring down at my face.

"Where's my stuff?"

"What?" I squeaked.

"Your friend. The fat one. He took my bag from the Diner."

I had no idea what he was talking about, but before I could even answer, Kevin came from nowhere and *CRACK!* laid Ned out with one punch. Ned fell like a sack of meat.

"No one fucks with my friends," Kevin said to the reeling giant. "No one."

We all scrambled to get into the car.

Spinning tires kicked up dust clouds as the Love Boat pulled out of the parking lot and we blew out onto the road.

Right on cue, Beef hung out the window, pumped his arms, and screamed, "Rock and …ooof!"

Kevin had had enough of this antic and promptly closed the passenger window on Beef's pink round belly.

A hand slides an 8-track into the car stereo.

Music blares from the speakers.

'I've seen the needle and the damage done
A little part of it in everyone

Every junkie's like a setting sun'

-Neil Young

DORCHESTER, MA – One Year Earlier

Jimmy Callahan looked thin. Thinner than usual.

It wasn't the stress that came on from caring for his aging mother, or the stress from his job as a high school European History teacher. He loved the students. He loved helping people understand other worlds. Escaping to the past was easy. It was more modern times, like the present, that Jimmy found difficult.

He and Kevin had that in common.

Where Kevin found his escape in music, Jimmy found his in drugs. Drugs were needed to numb his brain.

Painful memories of a life lived behind those lace curtains would fall on Jimmy like a mid-day August thunderstorm. Everything would be fine, and suddenly clouds would come rolling in, gathering force, and then bear down. They would howl and rage inside him, ripping him apart, ruining everything in its path, everything Jimmy thought could ever make him happy. And he would think to himself, 'Is there only pain and hatred and misery?'

Jimmy dropped the needle on an Elvis Costello album and Nick Lowe's lyrics spoke to his soul.

> *"And as I walked on*
>
> *Through troubled times*
>
> *My spirit gets so downhearted sometimes*
>
> *So where are the strong*
>
> *And who are the trusted?*

And where is the harmony?

Sweet harmony.

'Cause each time I feel it slippin' away, just makes me wanna cry

What's so funny 'bout peace love and understanding?

When the song ended, Jimmy gently slid the album into its sleeve and placed it into a box among the others.

Frampton Comes Alive. Born to Run. The Stranger.

His hand reached for something at the bottom of the box, hidden in the back behind The Rolling Stones *Exile on Main Street.*

A small bag of heroin.

Then Jimmy did what he sadly did all too often. He traded the record needle for the hypodermic one and allowed the drug to enter his vein and into his bloodstream. Drowning in the splendid weightlessness, he slowly began to drift away.

Away from Dorchester. Away from the McShanes. Away from his past. Away from his world and all its pain and hatred and misery. It was a warm and comforting escape.

Peaceful oblivion.

But escape was only temporary.

Storm clouds were always out there on the horizon.

****

Kevin walked into the Callahan home and found his friend strung out on the couch, the needles and drug paraphernalia strewn all over the table.

"Jesus Christ, Jimmy. How many times we gonna do this?!" Kevin said rushing to Jimmy's side.

There was no reaction. Jimmy was far away. Kevin grabbed him by the shoulders.

"You're a fuckin' teacher for Chrissake! Those kids look up to you. We all did."

Jimmy replied with a sad, lost, crooked smile.

"Norsemen, right?"

"That's right. The Norsemen," Kevin replied, happy to see his old friend remembered. "Come on, Jim. You're gonna kill yourself with this shit...and I may not be here to help again."

"Just leave me alone," Jimmy snapped, pulling away.

The back door slammed, signaling Old Man McShane had arrived home. Kevin looked at his drug addicted friend and shook his head.

"What are you still doin' in this fuckin' house, Jim? You should have left years ago."

"You mean like you?" Jimmy responded.

"The fuck's that supposed to mean?" Kevin said, sensing a change in Jimmy's mood.

Jimmy's expression darkened as he reached for the bag of poison on the table.

"You don't get it, do you?" he said. "Just go."

Kevin was at the end of his rope. They'd been through this drill too many times. He grabbed the Carlton Fisk baseball bat that was leaning against a nearby bookcase.

"Maybe I should crack your fuckin' skull and knock some sense into you. Is that what you want? I gave up everything to stay around here and help you!"

"Fuck you!" Jimmy shouted. The forcefulness of the words shook Kevin.

Jimmy knew Kevin better than anyone. He knew there was no coming back now. It had to be said, so he said it.

"You didn't stay for me. You were just too much of a pussy to leave." Then after a moment, Jimmy said, "I'm tired of being your fucking excuse."

The words hit Kevin like a punch to the gut.

He stood staring at the wreck of a man in front of him. Was it even Jimmy anymore? The Jimmy who grew up with him on the same block? The Jimmy who went to the same grammar school, the same church, the same middle school and high school?

No. The Jimmy Callahan he knew was gone.

"Go ahead, kill yourself," was the last thing Kevin said to his childhood friend. "I can't do this anymore."

He laid the baseball bat on the floor at Jimmy's feet and walked out.

A few minutes later, Old Man McShane entered the living room, evil and drunk, his shadow falling across the floor.

"Must be rackin' up quite a tab with me boys," he said glancing at the drugs on the table with disgust.

Jimmy sat up, defeated, and began to unfold a neatly wrapped cocktail napkin from the Eire Pub to get more heroin.

"Stickin' that shit in your arm aint gonna make your dead daddy come back, boyo," McShane snarled like the prick that he was.

Jimmy looked at his arm, at the Celtic Cross scar that was burnt onto his flesh as a teenager. The scar spread from pain and embarrassment to hatred and rage. He grabbed the bat at his feet and jammed it against the old man's throat.

They struggled.

McShane fell to the couch.

Jimmy cocked the bat back and glared at the old Irish prick with fury and hatred and rage in his eyes, the likes of which his world had never known. One good swing and he could end it all. One good swing would make all the storm clouds disappear. Gone forever.

But he couldn't do it.

Jimmy dropped the bat to his side.

He turned and walked away.

Seeing his chance, McShane rose from the couch. He pulled a knife out of his back pocket and lunged, about to strike.

Then, *BAM!*

Kevin pounced from out of nowhere.

McShane swung the knife wildly, cutting Kevin on the chest. A thin trail of blood formed and began to pool on his shirt. McShane moved in close and held the knife to Kevin's throat.

"Shoulda done this a long time ago," the Irish prick sneered.

Kevin looked at McShane.

Then *through* him.

Beyond him.

Kevin's eyes grew wide, as if they were saying, *'Do it. DO IT!'*

Suddenly, the bat rose from behind.

BOOM! McShane fell to the floor. Kevin looked at the 'Louisville Slugger' in shock.

It was Jimmy.

He stood motionless for what seemed like an eternity, then ran out the door with the bloodied Carlton Fisk baseball bat still in his hand.

Kevin crouched beside McShane's slumped body, breathless, unsure what to do.

A shadow emerged.

A voice, cold and clear and resolute instructed him.

"Put it in the Navy Yard," was all Mrs. Callahan said.

A hand slides an 8-track into the car stereo.

Music blares from the speakers.

*"And I can't get it out of my head
No, I can't get it out of my head
now my whole world is gone for dead
'cause I can't get it out of my head"*

-Electric Light Orchestra

DINER – UPSTATE NEW YORK

Kevin sat alone in the driver's seat and tried to shake the memory from his head. He's played the scene over and over and every time it ends the same way.

Jimmy taking off with the bat.

Mrs. Callahan coldly giving instructions.

Kevin disposing of Old Man McShane.

The sad reality was this wasn't the first time a dead body was in the trunk of the Love Boat.

Kevin flipped on the car radio (*finally*) and craned his neck to make sure no one could see him, because, holy shit, he genuinely liked the song that was on! (The guys told me it was a Britney Spears tune. Hehe.)

"What'cha listening to there, Top 40?" Joe said hopping into the back seat with Beef.

The two of them had just come back from the Diner. Beef was still angry about Joe taking that last creampuff, so we promised him we'd stop on the way back.

"What?! No!" Kevin replied quickly turning off the radio station.

"My kid likes this crap," he said, then added, "it's not half bad, I guess."

After a moment, Kevin began to confess.

"We don't really connect, ya know? It's just...his taste in music. Jesus H. Christ. It's brutal!"

"You do realize the first sign you're getting is old is when you hate your kid's music," Joe told him. "Which basically means my father was old his entire life."

"He's a teenager, Kev," Beef said. "It's his job not to connect with his father."

Kevin could feel it. Sitting there in the driver's seat of his beloved Bonneville. He was getting old.

We all were.

Twenty years passed faster than a race car on a speedway. One minute you're eighteen, invincible, staying up all night drinking beer, listening to Led Zeppelin, then in the blink of an eye you're middle-aged doing your best to stay awake past ten o'clock and you can't do any fun shit because you pulled a muscle in your back trying to put on your fucking socks.

Kevin stared out the window.

"I just wish Billy and I were closer. Sometimes I hear myself. I sound like my old man, and that scares the shit outta me. I just thought everything was gonna turn out different, ya know? He doesn't even call me Dad," Kevin said to us with a mixture of hurt and sadness. "Calls me 'Bro'."

"Just keep trying. Don't give up, he'll come back to you someday," Beef said. "Spend some time with him. I bet you two have a lot more in common than you think."

"That's what I'm afraid of. He says I live too much in the past. Sheila always did too. Not many wives stand by has-been high school football stars...even if they do have impeccable taste in music," Kevin said trying to be brave and mask his sadness.

He turned his head towards the Diner.

"I'm sure Katie would have felt the same way."

Beef and Joe looked at each other in the back seat, sharing the exact same thought.

"I'm a Townie," Kevin admitted. "Always will be. And I'm fine with that. Mike got Katie out of Dorchester. Palm trees and mansions instead of wrenches and car grease. She deserved to have that."

"You ever tell Mike, you know, about…?" Beef started, but Kevin stopped him

"No. And don't you either."

Kevin looked out past the Diner, as if he was having a vision.

"Ya know, best day of my life was when his book came out. I thought, that's it, everybody will finally realize Mike's just a Goddamn phony, and Katie will come running back to Boston. But that didn't happen. She loves him….in a way she never loved me."

His mood changed.

"Mr. Fuckin' *'GIMME 5!'* He's probably bangin' the maid back home."

"Maybe that's why they're getting divorced," Beef said.

"What?" Kevin exclaimed, spinning his head towards Beef.

"Nothing," Joe said, punching Beef on the arm.

"*Steven?*" Kevin said.

Uh oh. He used Beef's real name. Beef knew he meant business. It was a tone that reminded him of Sister Lucille our seventh-grade teacher at St. Marks. She would say our full name and use that sort of 'sing-songy' tone whenever someone was in trouble.

Beef was in trouble.

He cracked. "I can't...he...*I hate secrets!*"

"Mike asked us not to say anything," Joe admitted. "He just didn't want to deal with it."

"Deal with what?" Kevin asked.

"You three have history, and, well, you can be a little nostalgic sometimes," Joe said, treading lightly.

"*Nostalgic?* The fuck does that mean?" Kevin snapped.

"It's a nice way of saying you're a bit *obsessed*. You know. About the past, and stuff," Beef told him.

"There's that word again," Kevin barked. "I'm not obsessed!"

"Well, you're not 'Glen Close boiling bunnies' obsessed, but you do have a sort of can't-let-go-of-the-past edginess," Joe said looking down at Kevin's vinyl case of 8-tracks.

Kevin pulled the case close to his chest and held it tight like Linus with his security blanket.

"*Nostalgic,*" he muttered. "Fuck all of you."

Joe looked at his watch and Glumly grumbled, "We'll never make it."

Kevin was right. Everything was supposed to turn out different. At least it was supposed to be for Kevin and Katie.

It's amazing how you can spend a lifetime. Days and months and years go by without a hiccup and then it only takes one night, one bad decision to set the universe off its axis and change the course of everything.

A hand slides an 8-track cassette into the car stereo.

Music plays from the speakers.

"Why can't you just get it through your head
It's over, it's over now
Yes, you heard me clearly now I said
It's over, it's over now"

-Boz Scaggs

****

Kathleen Genevieve Fitzgerald was from a large devoutly Catholic Irish family, which meant a few things. No meat on Fridays. No missing Mass on Sundays. And no sex on Saturdays.

Or *any* days before marriage.

If the guilt of her religion didn't stop her from having premarital sex, then the fear of her three older brothers and father did.

Katie's father was nice enough, in a passive-aggressive biting-toned kind of way. He was the kind of man that would ask questions he already knew the answers to, like, "You're not wearing that out, are you?" knowing full well Katie would immediately run upstairs and change.

To Mr. Fitzgerald, everything was practical and for a purpose, the kind of guy who always utilized that top shirt breast pocket. The thing was always full of pens and a spare set of glasses at the ready in case they were ever needed. He raised his family the same way. To be practical and have purpose. It wasn't that Mr. Fitzgerald disliked Kevin, he just wanted more for his daughter than to be a Dorchester stereotype.

So did Katie.

After Katie found out that Kevin had turned down his scholarship to Holy Cross and planned on staying in Dorchester, things in their relationship sailed downhill pretty fast.

A few weeks later, one of the guys in the neighborhood had a bunch of people over. Danny Flynn's parents had gone away for the weekend, so it was the perfect place for a group of teenagers to sneak beers and act stupid. Once the party got going and the beer bottles piled up, Katie and Kevin started arguing. I'm not sure what it was about, but Katie got pretty upset and left. And Kevin did what he does best with relationship confrontation - he ran in the opposite direction.

Sheila Doherty was from Southie and had crossed town lines that night to attend the party. Most Southie girls were much 'faster' than the girls we knew, and Sheila ran laps around Katie in the waiting-till-marriage-to-have-sex department. She saw an easy target in Kevin that night. Who better to hook up with than the gridiron pride of Dorchester?

After Katie stormed out, Kevin got drunk. Real drunk. Then he got angry. And he got stupid.

When Sheila showed a sexual interest, Kevin was suddenly the high school football star again. Loved. Invincible. 'Chick arrogant.' And in his drunken state of mind, he convinced himself that he deserved it. 'Hey, I paid my dues. I've been faithful to Katie all through high school. Fuck her.'

When Katie came back to the party, she found Sheila and Kevin on the couch in the basement.

She ran to my house, crying and hurt beyond words.

Katie and I walked and talked for hours until the sun rose over the Boston skyline. That night, and for the first time, the streets of Dorchester looked shabby and dark and unpromising to the both of us. We found our common bond, and in that we found love.

A few weeks later, Sheila let Kevin know she was late.

Like, pregnant late.

So, Kevin 'did the right thing,' as the saying goes

They tried, at the beginning, and did all the things they were supposed to in marriage. Had a church ceremony. Christened the baby. Worked jobs. Ate dinner together. But they hardly knew each other. They had no history or anything in common between them. To make matters worse, Sheila loved Donna Summer, and Kevin *despised* Donna Summer. Especially the *Live and More* album. (Every Southie girl played that at parties in '78. 'A disco rendition of MacArthur's Park?! *'Someone left the cake out in the rain?'* What the fuck does that even mean?' Kevin would rant).

Sheila and Kevin were doomed from the start.

In fairness to them, reality just set in. That happens sometimes in relationships. Kevin described it once, as only Kevin could, in musical terms. He said it was sort of like going to a concert at the old Boston Garden. The place is rocking at the beginning. Balloons fall from the ceiling, everyone is singing and happy, and then just as quickly as it started, the music stops. The concert is over and all the lights in the stadium come on, and all is revealed. And suddenly you realize that you're just standing in a cold concrete building full of empty cups and cigarette butts, all ugly and unpleasant and cold.

Relationships can be like that if you let them.

In the end, Kevin and Sheila just couldn't make a marriage, or anything even resembling a marriage, work.

Sheila met a guy. Steve Healy from Quincy. Nice enough dude. Kevin couldn't stand him, of course. Not because he's with his ex-wife or gets to spend time with his son Billy, but because he's one of those guys who shouts '*So good, So good, So good*' during Sweet Caroline even when he's not at Fenway Park.

In typical Kevin fashion, his whole life played out in a song.

They got a divorce as a matter of course
and they parted the closest of friends.
Then the king and the queen went
back to the green but you can never go back
there again'

❖❖❖❖

I was inside the Diner chatting up a very blond and very young waitress while the guys were waiting in the car. She was legal, but young. I know, I know, it sounds kind of creepy and I'm still technically married, but it's all about my ego.

What you need to know at this point is that I didn't realize the ORDER HERE microphone was on and everyone in the parking lot could hear me.

The guys made running commentary from the car.

"So, do you know who I am?" I leaned in and asked the young waitress. My voice bellowed over the loudspeaker into the parking lot.

"Leave her alone," Kevin shouted from inside the car. "She has homework tonight!"

"With crayons!" Joe added.

"Have you read my book?" my smarmy voice boomed.

"I doubt it. There ain't any pictures," Kevin laughed.

"You know, 'The 5 Point Plan?'" I said, all full of my bullshit bravado.

"She can't count that high," Joe remarked

"Must be close to recess time," Kevin added.

"Jeeze. This is like watching a puppy on the highway. Somebody help that poor girl," Beef said, and they all enjoyed a big laugh.

Then, Kevin suddenly stopped laughing. Ned and Chester were pulling into the parking lot.

They had one deer strapped on the back of the truck and another one tied to the hood.

"Jesus Christ, does PETA know about these two?" Joe remarked as the hunters climbed out of their truck and entered the Diner. Joe noticed the bumper sticker on their tailgate that read: IF JESUS HAD A GUN HE'D BE ALIVE TODAY.

"Lovely," he said. "Well, this should be interesting."

As I chatted up the young waitress, my eyes caught the television playing in the corner of the Diner. Scrolling across the bottom of the screen was: **RABID ABBA FANS BREAK INTO THE ROCK AND ROLL HALL OF FAME**.

Seems our old security guard pal Lenny Palmer was on TV telling a Reporter that three men jumped him, broke into the Hall, and destroyed the ABBA exhibit.

"These guys must really hate ABBA," Lenny said to the reporter as I watched, "because the whole display is ruined. Just ruined! It's a real shame."

Lenny was convincing, but I knew the truth. Both about the 'alleged' break in and his deep hatred for ABBA.

The reporter looked into the camera and added, "Police tell us one of the suspects is Celebrity Life Coach Mike Crowley. With his latest book a massive failure, apparently it seems that Mike has turned to a life of vandalism."

The screen cut to one of my cheesy infomercials. In the ad, I'm speaking to a studio audience.

"Live life your own way. By your own code. And use my 5 Point Plan for Success," I said to the studio audience, then shouted each point in succession. "*Honesty. Loyalty. Courage. Discipline. Fidelity. GIMME 5!*"

The crowd erupted. "*GIMME 5!*"

I stared at the television. There was something about this particular ad on this particular day. It was as if I'd heard my own words for the very first time. They were familiar, but I couldn't quite place them.

My TV trance was broken when I saw Ned and Chester enter the Diner. I immediately bolted for the back door by the kitchen, then ran across the parking lot and dove headfirst through the passenger window into the Love Boat.

"We got problems in there, boys," I said straightening out my legs.

"We got problems out here too," Beef replied.

"The police are looking for us," I told them. "They said we were ABBA fans and broke into the Hall of Fame."

Kevin was apoplectic.

"What the fuck? I'm not an ABBA fan!"

I could see the waitress inside, pointing Ned towards our direction.

"Start the car, Kev," Joe said as calmly as he could. "I think you really pissed off Elmer Fudd in there."

"I can't afford to get arrested," Beef pleaded.

"The paparazzi are gonna have a field day with this!" I said, totally pissed off.

Ned left the Diner and started to walk towards the car.

"Just keep your shit together," Kevin replied fumbling with the keys. "We didn't do anything illegal."

"Well, the dead body in the trunk may need some explaining," Joe replied.

Ned was almost at the car.

"Just go, Kevin," I said in a high-pitched voice. "Go!"

He turned the key.

Nothing.

Not even a click.

"Come on girl. Not now. Come on," Kevin said trying to coax the Love Boat engine to turn over.

"Open the Goddamn door, Masshole!" Ned growled, grabbing the passenger door handle.

"Fuck you!" Kevin yelled across the seat over a petrified and completely sweat-soaked Beef.

"Come on, girl...Come on..." Kevin pleaded.

The engine fired and missed.

Kevin pounded his fist on the steering wheel and screamed, "COME ON!"

The engine turned.

"GM really needs to revisit this model," Joe said calmly, almost as if he were enjoying the danger. Me on the other hand? I was a mess. My heart was beating in my chest and I don't remember ever being so scared.

Just then, the young waitress came running towards the car, finally recognizing who I was.

"Get outta the fuckin' way!" Kevin yelled at her.

"Hey, don't talk to my fan base like that!" I shouted at him.

Ned raced back to his truck. He grabbed his shotgun, cocked it and raised it in our direction, but the waitress was in the way.

"Stay in the fuckin' way! Stay in the fuckin' way!" Joe screamed in a high-pitched shrill, clearly not enjoying this anymore.

Kevin shifted into drive.

The waitress jumped aside.

Ned hopped into his truck and headed towards us, his oversized tires screaming rubber atop the pavement. The truck cut us off, blocking our path. As Ned slammed the brakes, the deer *FLEW* off the roof of his truck. It crashed onto the hood of the Love Boat with a *THUD* landing eyeball to eyeball with Beef. He screeched like a pre-teen girl.

"Ahhh! I'm a vegetarian!"

We all looked at him in shock.

Joe just shook his head, enjoying the revelation.

"Fuckin' irony, man. And the hits just keep on comin'."

Kevin dropped the gearshift into reverse. The engine screamed and the Love Boat tires spun as the car lurched back and the deer slid off the hood, now blocking Ned's truck.

As we pulled away, Beef hung out the window, pumped his arms and screamed, "Rock and Roll!"

Then got hit directly on the forehead with bird shit.

BOSTON POLICE DEPARTMENT

Sergeant Tom Powers was an eager-to-please cop with gull white hair that made him automatically seem older than he was. He sat across Detective Kelly's cluttered desk awaiting instructions.

"How long you been on the force now, Powers?" Kelly asked.

"About eight years," Powers replied.

Kelly leaned forward and reached for the baseball perched on the corner of his desk. He slowly spun it in his hand, looking closely at the seams and tightly bound leather as it seemed to evoke memories.

"My first few years on the force didn't pay much, so we had to hustle to grab extra pay," Kelly said, reminiscing about the old days. "I was able to pick up overtime shifts working security at Fenway. Sweet gig. We had access to the dugout. Left field wall. The locker rooms. Players were great. Dewey Evans. Yaz. Bill Lee. Carlton Fisk. No big salaries and big egos back then. They were always pleasant, giving us extra souvenirs. Hats...balls....bats."

Kelly pulled a cigar box from the desk drawer. He reached in and showed Sergeant Powers a black and white photo of two young police cadets.

"That's me and Bill Callahan. We grew up together. Same Parish. Went to BC High and UMass. Then we graduated the Academy together. Good cop. Salt of the earth guy. A Foxhole kinda friend, you know what I mean?"

"I guess," Powers replied weakly.

"Jesus," Kelly sighed, staring deeply at the photo. "Do people even have friendships like that anymore?"

He leaned back and spun the baseball in his hand.

"Bill wanted to take his kid to a Sox game, so he asked me to trade shifts. Just a routine traffic detail on Morrissey Boulevard."

Kelly stopped to catch himself before continuing. Officer Powers could see the shift in the grizzly veteran detective's mood. It was clear that it still pained him.

"Bill was dead when I got there. Drunk driver. Guy never hit the brakes. Thing is... I was late relieving him. Coulda' been me pinned under that car."

Powers didn't know what to say.

"Kid was waiting outside the bleachers when I told him, two tickets in his hand," Kelly said, took a moment to collect himself.

He didn't want to seem weak or melancholy.

But he was.

"Bill's wife remarried. Jimmy needed a father. McShane needed a Green Card. I guess she thought she was doing the right thing."

"McShane?" Powers replied, a bit taken aback. "As in, dead-in-the-Navy-yard-McShane?"

The mention of the name seemed to pain Richie Kelly.

"They both took a ton of shit from that prick McShane, but divorce was never an option. It's what good Catholic wives did back then. Shut up and make the best of it. They'd stay in that lousy married because of community, religion, tradition. Whatever. And sometimes because they just didn't have any other choice."

Detective Kelly shook off the weak melancholy and got back to police business.

"Buddy of mine just called from the State Police. They pulled a hearse over for speeding in upstate New York."

"Really? What's the hurry? Guys already dead," Officer Powers replied trying to lighten the mood.

"It's more a 'missing person' than a moving violation," Kelly replied, not at all amused at the weak joke.

"Bill's son is in that hearse. Jimmy. Or he was supposed to be, anyway. He died in Cleveland a few days ago. Heroin. Funeral Home was transporting the body. The Trooper searched the vehicle and found an empty casket. Driver almost shit himself."

Kelly opened a large manila envelope and spilled surveillance pictures onto the desk between them. Beef's Deli. Sullivan's Garage. The Erie Pub.

"I have a pretty good idea who's bringing him in," Kelly said. "Called themselves The Norsemen. Bastards stole my Crown Vic when they were in high school. Fucked up all my easy-listening pre-set buttons. I could have arrested them, and their lives would have changed. But I've seen enough of that on the streets of Dorchester."

Richie Kelly knew that loyalty was part of the fabric of the Dorchester streets. Friendships are thick. Sometimes thicker than family.

He looked up at Officer Powers and said, "I want you to greet them all when they get back."

SOMEWHERE UPSTATE NEW YORK

We drove the Bonneville through the backroads of upstate New York in silence for most of the night. We were all getting tired and cranky as the beer, fast food and lack of sleep began to take its toll on our middle-aged bodies.

Joe and Beef started to push and kick at each other like little kids in the back seat, which annoyed the piss out of an already cranky Kevin.

"Cut the shit back there," he yelled from behind the wheel.

Joe looked at his watch and grumbled for the millionth time, "We'll never make it."

"Jesus Christ, will you shut up already!" Kevin barked. "We'll make it!"

"No, we won't," Joe whispered loudly.

"Yes, we will!" Kevin shouted.

A loud *BANG* came from the engine.

We all looked at each other.

"Ok. So, we might be a little late," Kevin admitted.

He pulled the car to the side of the road and shut off the engine, not that there was any fear of other cars whizzing by this lonely, woodsy stretch of road.

"This is great. Just great. Now we're stuck on some stupid country back road," I groaned.

"You're the one who told me to get off the highway!" Kevin yelled, the veins in his neck looking like they were about to pop.

"I'm trying to avoid the Paparazzi!" I said, and honestly thought Kevin was going to kill me.

Some guys would cherish these moments. Getting back together with old friends. Making memories. The excitement of danger. Cruising along on the open road of adventure.

I am not one of those people.

In fact, we all were at the end of our ropes.

"So, what now? We sleep out here and wait?" Beef weakly asked.

"Fuck that," Joe said. "We've come too far as a society for me to sleep outdoors. That's why I hate campers. Frankly, I think it's rude to our forefathers who died in cold, dark woods just like these so we could sleep and shit indoors."

"So, you don't poop or pee in the woods either?" Beef asked. (*Poop. Pee.* Classic Beef. Never a curse word.)

"I'm not that much of a patriot," Joe said, then took off for the back of the hearse to relieve himself.

Kevin gave a resigned sigh and ran his hand over the dashboard.

"I guess the Love Boat's just getting too old for these road trips."

"So are we. Explain to me again why we couldn't just let the driver bring Jimmy back?" I asked.

"Because it was the right thing to do. And apparently," Kevin said glaring at Beef in the rearview mirror to punch the word, "it's *nostalgic.*"

"Nostalgic? What the hell does that even mean?" I asked.

Kevin gave a heavy sigh.

"I have no idea. But we all agreed to one last road trip. Like old times. Like high school."

As if right on cue, Joe appeared at the windshield shaking the bag of weed that we took from Jimmy's locker.

"Well boys," he said with that wry ironic smile of his. "If we're gonna do it like high school, we might as well do it right."

A hand slides an 8-track cassette into the car stereo.

Music plays from the speakers.

"Here I am, on a road again
There I am, up on the stage
Here I go, playing star again
There I go, turn the page"

-Bob Seger

****

The four of us sat against the hood of the Love Boat passing a joint like we were teenagers again, leaning against our old Dory rowboat and staring at a bonfire. My cell phone vibrated, and for the first time in a long time I ignored it.

Joe looked at his watch and said with a high-as-a-kite confident smile, "We got plenty of time."

"Road trip. Beers. Weed. This all feels familiar," I said.

"It's all good," Joe nodded.

"Except for the lack of sufficient munchies," Beef slurred.

"And the cops," I added.

"And the dead-body-in-the-trunk thing," Joe reminded us.

Kevin, who had been distant and silent, finally spoke up.

"Jimmy should be here."

"He is, Kev," I told him. "In case you forgot, Jimmy's in the trunk."

"You know what I mean," Kevin said. "He could have been anything, and I let him end up a goddamn janitor at the Rock and Roll Hall of Fame. I mean, who the fuck pays forty bucks to look at ABBA's bell-bottoms?!"

Joe, who was really baked at this point, took another hit off the joint and began to ponder.

"How much you think they'd charge you to see Art Garfunkel's comb?"

"I just don't get why he left," I said.

"Elvis's toilet..." Joe philosophized.

"I mean, Jimmy would never leave his mother alone like that," I continued.

"Marvin Gaye's Father's Day cards..." Joe continued.

"He never even said goodbye," Beef said sadly.

"Freddy Mercury's unused dental retainer..."

"Will you shut the fuck up!" Kevin shouted, then shook his head. "What a disaster."

"I don't know, it's not all bad," Beef declared. "I got some pretty cool souvenirs out of it."

Kevin looked over at the rest of us and said sarcastically, "And this is what you guys left me with back in Dorchester. Happy?"

We all smiled.

I was finally relaxed, finally enjoying myself and my friends. Not to mention the weed.

"This feels good, bustin' balls," I admitted. "You know, I've made a fortune writing books. All these lonely people out there, searching for friendship. They'd give anything to have what we have. It's so...easy."

I looked down and stared at my feet for a moment. "It's everything else that's hard work."

I let the words sit out there and sink in a bit.

You know how every now and then you have a moment where your whole life stretches out in front of you? You know who you are and why you're there, and everything seems clear and perfect?

This was one of those moments.

Like our last bonfire on Cape Cod.

"Do you know I haven't made one real friend since high school?" I admitted to them. "We go to these bullshit parties. I look around and within seconds I know without even meeting them - this one's an asshole, this one's a prick, this one's a loser. Katie and I used to have dinner friends, neighbors I'd borrow shit from, but there's no one like you guys. I realize that now. Your first true friends shape who you are. The ground rules are set. You just instinctively know what's funny and how far to push things. Then we get older. Along the way you meet a few people with some of the same traits, but it's never the whole package. There's just something about the people who knew you growing up."

Joe couldn't let the moment pass without busting my balls and said, "Why do I get the feeling I'm gonna hear this on my TV at three in the morning?"

Kevin looked at me, his face full of knowing accusation.

"Wait. What do you mean you and Katie *used* to have friends?"

I looked at him.

"Katie and I are getting a divorce, Kev. Well, we were supposed to. That's the meeting I missed back in LA."

"But you're still wearing your wedding ring," Beef pointed out.

"Yeah," I replied full of my usual, smarmy cockiness. "LA women are attracted to married guys."

"Jesus Christ, you haven't changed a fuckin' bit," Kevin snapped. "No wonder Katie's leaving you."

"I haven't changed?!" I snapped back. "You still listen to 8-tracks and drive a '74 Bonneville!"

"Hey, let's leave the Love Boat out of this," a fully baked Joe interjected.

I was really pissed off.

"It's like this whole road trip was supposed to be some kind of magic time warp. You're the one who needs to grow up, Kevin. Let go of the past and get a life. I did!"

Kevin didn't miss a beat.

"Like we should all listen to you? Big shot TV personality. Of course people buy your books. What loser watching TV at 3 AM *doesn't* need a friend?! And my car is a classic. A nice memory. You should try it sometime, Mike, but it might remind you that you were just a pimple faced loser who couldn't wait to get away. Tell that to the Paparazzi if they ever show up."

"Come on guys, that's enough," Beef said, always the one trying to keep the peace.

"Yeah," Joe added. "We all know Mike's face cleared up Junior year."

No one laughed.

The tension was too thick, emotions too high.

I turned and faced Kevin.

"You know what? You're right, I was a pimple-faced loser. But I moved on and did something with my life, instead of hanging on and living in the past. You didn't even try. So, who's the real loser, Kev? And let's be honest here, you're still mad because I'm the one who got Katie."

"And you lost her! You lost everything. *I* should let go of the past? At least I didn't package it up and sell it! I love how you actually think politics gave you your Five Point Plan. *'GIMME 5!'* Give me a fucking break! You used us, Mike. All of us. The Norsemen. You sold our friendship for chapters in some fucking bullshit discounted self-help book."

Kevin pointed a thumb at each of us.

To Beef.

"Honesty."

To Joe.

"Loyalty."

To Jimmy in the car.

"Courage."

Then finally, to himself.

"*Discipline,*" he said, then glared at Joe and Beef. "Which we all know is just a code word for obsessed."

Joe whispered, "I woulda gone with nostalgic there."

Kevin continued. "And of course, Point 5. The shining example of *Fidelity* himself. Mike Crowley. The cheatin', stealin' prick."

"Come on, Kevin. Stop it," Beef pleaded.

"No. Fuck him and his Hollywood good looks and morally superior attitude. How many affairs have you had, Mike? How many nameless book groupies have you banged? No wonder Katie's divorcing you!"

Joe spoke up.

"Okay, everybody settle down. You have any Barry Manilow in that case? I think we could all use a little 'Mandy' right about now."

I slumped against the car, feeling as if I'd been punched in the gut. For the first time in my life, I was speechless. Kevin was right. My Five Point Plan *was* describing each of them. I guess I blocked it out. Just like I blocked out growing up in a run-down triple-decker from the lower-class section of Dorchester. I borrowed the idea from Jimmy and his Viking Virtues. (*The **Nine Noble Virtues** of Norse Paganism are Courage, Truth, Honour, Fidelity, Discipline, Hospitality, Self-Reliance, Industriousness, Perseverance)

Okay, so borrowed wouldn't be the right word, exactly. Stole. I stole them.

Well, five of them, anyway.

"I... I had to come up with something," I confessed. "My political career was dead. I didn't know what else to do. Maybe I just didn't want to remember."

And then, it all became clear.

I remembered everything.

I remembered being young and strong and happy.

I looked directly at Kevin.

"But I remember this. I remember a time when you were all those qualities. Every single one of them. Now you're just old and bitter. And just to be clear, I've never cheated on Katie. *Ever.*"

After a moment, I confessed.

"I'm the one who filed the papers. Katie cheated on me."

The guys were stunned. Kevin more than the others. He looked hurt, and I sort of felt sorry for him.

"I think she slept with the pool boy," I sadly admitted.

"The pool boy?" Joe said, still high. "How fucking Hollywood is that?!"

"How come I never knew they had a pool?" Beef whispered.

Joe grabbed the joint away from him in disgust and said, "The pond would be better for you."

"Part of me doesn't blame her if she did," I admitted. "I've been caught up in myself for so long. Sometimes I just want to feel young again, you know what I mean?"

I think that resonated. We all wanted to feel that way again.

"You guys. You were my closest friends," I said. "But Katie? Katie's my *best* friend. And I pushed her away."

"You said *if*. Like, you think *maybe* she cheated?" Kevin asked. "Trust me, kid. Katie would never be with another guy."

"How do you know?" I asked.

"I know, because... I tried," he replied.

My initial confusion quickly turned to rage. I leapt at Kevin, but Beef grabbed my arm and held me back.

"Nothing happened, I swear," Kevin began. "Katie was in town. You were away on some book tour. Sheila had just left me. I...I was hammered and..."

I didn't care. I broke free and tackled Kevin to the ground.

Beef and Joe jumped in to try and stop the fight. All four of us rolled on the ground, swinging, slapping, fighting until, exhausted, we broke apart and sat in silence.

We had officially hit rock bottom.

We all just sat there, not sure what to do or what to say.

Joe finally spoke.

"So, just to be clear. When I die, I want to be cremated."

"Fuck you," me and Kev yelled in unison.

There was a long silence until Kevin raised his head and looked right at me.

"She loves you, Mike. Plain and simple. Katie would never do anything to hurt you. You know that. I'm sorry I did."

He stood over me, stuck out a hand and winked, "C'mon. *GIMME* 5!"

"God, I hate that fucking saying," I said.

Kevin helped me up and we held the handshake for a few seconds until we both knew we were going to be okay.

That is, until a figure appeared from the woods.

"Well, well, well. If it ain't the ABBA-lovin' Massholes."

It was Ned.

And he was pointing his shotgun directly at us.

SULLIVAN AUTO REPAIR – DORCHESTER, MA

The west coast lifestyle agreed with Katie. Her body was firm and tanned, a nice mixture of LA fitness and Irish genetics. She climbed out of a Ford Taurus and called out to the teenager at the other side of the garage.

"Billy? My God, you're so grown up. It's Katie Crowley. I mean, Fitzgerald. Katie Fitzgerald. Your dad's old..." she corrected herself. "Your dads friend."

"Oh hey, Mrs. Crowley. You must be in town for the funeral," Billy replied. He looked the car up and down. "Shouldn't you be, like, driving a Porsche or something?"

"The Porsche is Mike's. You know, *Mr. 5 Point Plan*," she said half mocking and half embarrassed by my celebrity.

"This is my father's," Katie replied. "It's nice to be in a town where people don't give a shit about the kind of car you drive, ya know?"

"Oh, I know," Billy replied. "My dad still drives the Bonneville. Some things never change, huh?"

Katie's eyes scanned the garage and fell on a pile of old 8-tracks. She smiled, but there was a faraway look on her face.

"Yes. Unfortunately, they do," she replied with a heavy sigh,

Her eyes found an old Polaroid prom photo taped to the wall, just like the one from Kevin's visor. Powder blue tuxedo Kevin and Gunny sack dress Katie. She leaned in close to the photo.

"Jesus, look at us," she said, her eyes small and searching, wondering. She was far away.

"Your Grandmother took this picture. She was a hot shit. Tough as nails, too. They all were. My mother. Mrs. Sullivan. Mrs. Callahan. What a crew. Back then, every Dorchester girl's dream was to marry a fireman or a cop, get a triple decker, live in the same parish they grew up in and have kids. They never left. Ever."

And she was right. That *was* every girl from the neighborhood's dream. But not Katie's. She peeled off from that tired life dream a long time ago. And certainly not mine.

We had that in common. We both wanted more.

I like to think that Katie and I were meant to be together, more than her and Kevin ever were. Even if Kevin hadn't cheated with Sheila that night at Danny Flynn's party, I think Katie and I would have found each other.

Truth is, I always loved her. And I think she always loved me.

At least she used to.

Katie fished into her pocket for a cigarette.

I never liked it when she would smoke at our home in Malibu, but she always kept a pack hidden somewhere. She would always fall back into that bad habit as soon as she came home to Boston. City girl to the core. 'You can take the girl out of Dorchester' as the saying goes.

Katie fired up her cigarette and took a long pull.

There was a Boston Police business card lying among the 8-tracks. She read it aloud.

"'Detective Richard Kelly'. Detective now, huh?"

"He was here a few days ago asking my dad a bunch of questions. He seemed pretty shook up about it," Billy told her.

Katie grinned at a memory.

"Kelly's probably still pissed. The boys stole his Crown Vic back in high school. He loved that car," she said, then looked at Billy with a smirk. "You know the type. Really obsessed."

Billy smiled back. "Ha. Tell me about it. Can I ask you a question?"

"Sure."

"You think my dad would ever sell that car?"

"The Love Boat?" Katie said with an exaggerated shudder at the thought. "I seriously doubt it. Your great grandfather gave him that car. I remember how much that pissed your grandfather off."

"I heard," Billy replied, then looked away and down. "I think he cares more about that car and those stupid tapes than anything else."

Katie could feel the hurt in his voice. It was familiar. But she wasn't sure what to say or how to fix it. The same way she couldn't fix it when Kevin was a hurt teenager.

"So, where is Mr. Classic Rock?" she asked.

"He left. Said he needed to do something for Jimmy ...like always," Billy replied in a tone that didn't mask his hurt and jealousy.

And in that moment, Katie and Billy shared a unique connection; Kevin making Jimmy a priority. Apparently, that bond was still getting in the way of relationships.

Billy was right. Some things never change.

"Well, he must think pretty highly of you, leaving you in charge like this," Katie said thinking that might help.

"I guess," Billy shrugged.

Katie took another drag on the cigarette and noticed the splintered 8-track cassette still lying on the floor from her phone call delivering the news of Jimmy's death. She bent down and held the plastic case for Boz Scaggs *Silk Degrees* in her hand.

She was far away again, looking at her own unhappiness.

"Don't give up on him," she said. "I know he can be a real asshole sometimes, but he's really not that bad."

But Katie wasn't talking to Billy about his dad.

She was talking to herself.

About me.

"You know Bill, 'Love is a Battlefield.'" she said with a smirk. "Just don't tell your father. He hated Pat Benatar."

Then she did her best imitation of Kevin.

"Chicks can't sing."

Billy smiled big. It was easy to see why his dad kept that Polaroid photo all these years.

****

Detective Richie Kelly was a man of routines. Every morning he had a corn muffin with butter, no margarine, and a Dunkin' Donuts coffee. One sugar. No milk. No cream. 'You can never depend on dairy,' he'd say.

To Richie Kelly, life and people were put into 3 categories:

1. Sox vs Yankees.
2. Beatles vs Stones.
3. Dunkin Donuts vs Starbucks.

Kim Bletzer entered Kelly's office with a steaming cup of coffee. Starbucks. Grande Café Americano. Skim milk and two sugars. Of course. It was just another reason for Richie Kelly not to like her.

"Thought you might want to see this," Bletzer said with an air of cockiness.

She spun the computer monitor on his desk and began to type on the keyboard. A black and white surveillance video popped up on the screen of Joe, Beef and Mike running through the Rock and Roll Hall of Fame. Bletzer leaned back and gave Kelly time to take it all in.

"Now, what the hell do you think these Dot Rats are doing in Cleveland?" she said with a smug, knowing smirk.

"Maybe they love Rock and Roll," Kelly replied, trying to be a smartass.

"Or maybe they're just doing your job for you," Bletzer curtly replied.

She leaned forward and clicked to a new surveillance screen. This one was of Beef sitting alone in the maintenance room. With a few clicks of the mouse, Bletzer zoomed the camera in and they both watched as Beef reached into the metal locker and pulled out a bat.

A baseball bat.

The *Carlton Fisk* baseball bat.

Detective Kelly reacted hard. Shit!

Bletzer grabbed the Coroner's report still sitting on the desk.

"'Blunt trauma to the head,'" she read aloud. "I'd say that's your murder weapon right there. Just get that evidence and let's close this thing, Detective."

Bletzer dropped the folder back onto the desk, grabbed her Café Americano and walked out.

'Fuck her,' Kelly thought to himself. 'She's probably a Yankees and Stones fan too.'

Richie Kelly suspected all along that Jimmy might be involved in the McShane murder. But Jimmy was always too sensitive, too weak. Besides, that was the easy choice. The logical choice. And in Detective Richie Kelly's experience the logical choice was never the answer.

While the rest of the force was thinking drug deal gone bad or some overdue loan shark payment, Kelly knew it was something else.

And some*one* else.

Bludgeoning meant rage, and rage meant revenge. Revenge for a lifetime of abuse. Revenge for a life altered. Revenge seeded in anger and hate.

Richie Kelly had no intention of ever going after his buddy Bill Callahan's son. He had someone else in mind. He pulled a notepad from his desk and wrote down a name: **Kevin Sullivan.**

Kelly turned his eyes back to the computer screen, then clicked to another surveillance video. This one showed Lenny Palmer angrily destroying an exhibit of sequined jumpsuits and bell bottom costumes.

"Jesus Christ," he muttered, watching the ballistic security guard wreaking havoc on Benny's piano, Björn's guitars, Frida and Agnetha's microphones. "This guy really hates ABBA."

A hand slides an 8-track cassette into the car stereo.

Music plays from the speakers.

"So when you're near me,

*darling can't you hear me S. O. S.
The love you gave me,*

nothing else can save me S. O. S."

-ABBA

****

We stood silent and motionless, the moon casting a bright light among the trees, as Ned aimed his shotgun in our direction.

"Where's the bag?" Ned growled.

Joe pointed to the pile of souvenir gift bags piled along the Love Boat's back dash window.

"You're gonna have to be more specific," he said. "Beef's been a real shot in the arm for the local economy."

"You boys better pray it's not broken," Ned spat as he motioned Chester to retrieve it.

Kevin stepped in front, protecting us all from Ned's gun.

"We're cool, right? Everything's cool. This is all a big misunderstanding."

Beef stepped in front of Kevin.

"We were only trying to help our friend," he said.

Joe stepped in front, his arms spread wide, protecting us all. "Look guys. We really don't need any more dead bodies on this trip."

Ned and Chester look at each other. Dead bodies?

"He's in the car," Kevin told them.

"Actually, he's in the trunk," I piped up from the back.

Kevin walked over and popped the trunk, and we all stared at the thick black body bag.

"His mother wants him buried next to his prick stepfather," Kevin told them. "We're just trying to get our friend home so we can give him the funeral he'd want."

Ned stared for a moment then solemnly shook his head as if a great disservice had fallen upon him.

"Just like Gram Parsons," he sighed.

"Exactly," Kevin agreed, then, "Wait, what? You know about him?"

Big old deer hunter homophobic Ned finally softened. He looked at us all, crossed his massive arms in front of his chest and then looked the Love Boat up and down.

"What'chu got here, '73?"

"'74," Kevin replied. "Fan belt is busted."

"I think I can hook you up."

After a few minutes, the fan belt was replaced, and the Love Boat was ready to roll.

"Sorry about that punch. When you grabbed my friend...I...I, well I guess I have some anger issues," Kevin admitted.

"I hear ya," Ned replied. "Got some things I need to work on myself."

"Like rage," Joe said.

"Tolerance," I added.

"Violence," Beef said.

Chester joined in.

"Patience. Manners. Hygiene..."

"Okay, Okay. Shaddup, I get it!" Ned blurted. "You boys get your friend home. And no more playing ABBA. I fucking hate ABBA."

As Ned climbed in and sat behind the wheel of his truck, he gingerly opened the plastic souvenir bag on his lap and quickly checks the contents. Hunting knife. Camouflage hat. A GPS tracker. (So, that's how he was able to follow us!) His eyes suddenly gleamed and he cradled something in his hand as if he were delicately holding a newborn baby chick.

But it wasn't a newborn baby chick.

It was an 8-track cassette!

He placed it beside a pile of others on the front seat.

"Careful with those, you idiot!" he barked at Chester who was climbing in and disturbing the collection.

The three of us stared at Kevin in disbelief.

Oh. My. God.

Ned was officially Kevin's Doppelgänger.

As the truck drove away, Beef broke our trance.

"Guys, I have a confession to make."

"Jesus Christ, what now?" Kevin declared.

"I kinda like ABBA," Beef admitted.

"Me too," I said.

"Well, since we're all coming clean here," Joe said, then crouched down to reach under the seat of the Love Boat. Doing his best Dick Stockton play-by-play imitation from Game 6 of the '75 World Series, Joe announced, *"There it goes... long drive... If it stays fair... Home Run!"*

A long time ago, a lifetime ago, we were all friends. But all was about to go terribly wrong terribly fast.

Joe had Jimmy's bat.

The Carlton Fisk bat.

"What the fuck?!" Kevin said as a shadow of nervousness flashed across his face. "Where did you get that?"

"It's the bat that almost won them the Series. Must be worth a fortune now, right Beef?" Joe said in a tone full of accusation.

"It better be," Beef replied, grabbing the bat away.

We all stared at him, waiting for an explanation.

"I...I expanded the Deli and then, boom, the economy crashed. I needed some extra cash, so I started betting. It was just small stuff at first. Horses. Numbers. Then I missed a mortgage payment, and another. That store is my grandfather's. I can't be the one who loses it."

After a moment, he confessed.

"I'm in deep, guys. To the McShanes."

We were stunned.

This was bad.

Really, really bad.

"Jesus. Heroin and gambling," I said, dumbfounded.

"Nice to see they've moved beyond kneecaps and car bombs," Joe said breaking the tension. "Those boys certainly have a diversified portfolio."

"Why didn't you just ask us for help?" I said.

"Sure, you'd all love that, wouldn't you? Poor old Beef. *That*' Steven needs money. Well you know what...?"

Beef stopped and thought for a second. It was as if the word was stuck in his throat.

Finally, he blurted, "Fuck you guys!"

I'm not sure what we were most stunned about. The fact that Beef had the Carlton Fisk bat, that he owed money to the McShane's, or that he just used the 'F' word. (As he would say).

In that exact moment, it was almost as if Beef had grown up before our eyes. He was no longer a goofy man-child.

Beef turned red with anger and furiously swung the bat.

"You, the big celebrity. You, the Federal leg breaker!"

He grabbed for Kevin's case of tapes.

"You and your stupid 8-tracks!"

"No, Beef. No!!" Kevin yelled.

But it was no use, Beef was going off the rails, a man possessed.

"I'm not a loser," he shouted, his face knotted with rage and pity. "I'm not! And I'm not that fat!"

Joe grabbed him before he could get to the case, and we all wrestled Beef to the ground.

No one spoke for a few minutes. We were all too exhausted and too confused. Finally, Joe put an arm around our husky friend.

"Good thing you swing like a girl."

Beef smiled a sad little smile.

"The last time we sat around like this was the Cape after graduation. Everything was perfect."

He was right.

What the hell happened?

Kevin spoke up.

"Sorry I dragged you guys out here. I just, I don't know, I was hoping maybe we could capture what we had one more time, ya know? You're right Mike, I'm the one who never grew up. After Sheila left, I moved back home with my mother. How *'nostalgic'* is that?"

Joe looked at him.

"Well, Oedipus, I work for the Goddamn IRS...and I'm the one who hated math! All I do is probe assholes for a living."

After a moment, he asked, "What age do you let your dreams die? Thirty-five? Forty? Fifty? God, I hate my job."

We sat in dead silence. I just shook my head as a sad realization came to me.

"A janitor at the Rock and Roll Hall of Fame. Think about it, that's really perfect. Music and history. I bet Jimmy loved going to work every day. He was maybe the happiest one out of all of us. It's just too bad he didn't realize it."

We all took that in.

Kevin raised his head and looked at Beef.

"I'm gonna need that bat."

"Just let him keep it," Joe told him.

"You don't understand. I need to get rid of it."

And suddenly, Kevin looked different. I saw something in his expression.

"So, let me ask a question," I said raising a semi suspicious eyebrow. "How did Old Man McShane die again?"

"He got hit," Beef answered.

"No, I mean specifically," I said. "What was the cause of death?"

Sometimes, there are things you don't want to know the answers to.

This was one of those times.

Kevin glared at me. He knew what I was thinking. He answered my question deliberately and through gritted teeth.

"I think the official medical term was, 'a crack to his fuckin' head.'"

Then Kevin looked at each of us one by one, as if seeking some kind of justification and forgiveness.

"It had to end. You guys know that."

"Wait, you...?" Beef asked, his eyes wide.

"No. I didn't," Kevin assured us, then after a heavy pause said, "But I sure as hell didn't try to stop him."

There was a moment of shocked universal silence, then it all came clear. Now we knew, and the answer rocked us. It rocked all the way back to our beach at Lewis Bay on the Cape. All eyes were on Kevin as the harsh realization washed over the group.

"Jesus," Joe whispered. "So that's why Jimmy left..."

"We all knew what was going on," Kevin said. "We never did enough to stop it."

"We were just kids," I said, weakly.

"That's not an excuse," Joe said shaking his head.

And Joe was right.

"Wait. I don't get it," Beef said, confused as ever. "So, you don't think the bat's worth anything now?"

"It's not an eBay item, Beef. It's evidence," I said before turning my attention to Kevin. "That's why you wanted to go to Cleveland, isn't it?"

"I wasn't the only one who used this road trip as an excuse," Kevin answered, his words strong and measured, hitting us all right between the eyes.

And he was right, too.

Whether it was the bat or the money or the adventure or the escape, we each had our own selfish reasons for agreeing to come on this journey.

Kevin held his hand out to Beef.

"I need the bat."

"No," Beef snapped, and I think that may have been the first time any of us ever heard Beef refuse Kevin.

"We never lied to each other," he said. "***Ever.*** McShane is dead. Jimmy's dead. And the Norsemen...well, that's dead too."

Everything was out of balance.

Beef was suddenly sitting on all the power, and our heads were spinning. He was right, we were all falling away from each other. Jimmy was the glue that held us together, at least he did when we were kids. But that was the problem. We weren't kids anymore.

Joe spoke up.

"So, let me see if I can recap here. We have the cops looking for us in Cleveland. The McShanes waiting for us back in Dorchester. Two homicidal deer hunters. Breaking and entering at the Rock and Roll Hall of Fame. An Amish strip joint, which was weird on so many levels. One bag of weed. One stolen dead body. Did I miss anything?"

"The Louisville slugger murder weapon," I said, seething at Kevin.

"Oh yeah, thanks. Super. Just super," Joe replied. "I love these Class Reunions. Let's make sure we get the bat into the group photo."

"I can't believe this," I mumbled, shaking my head.

"I can't believe a lot of things, Mike," Beef said. "I can't believe you'd ever leave Katie. I can't believe we drove our dead friend four hundred miles."

He paused, then said sadly, "I can't believe how we all changed."

"I can't believe you're a vegetarian," Joe added.

"This was a mistake," Kevin said then walked around to the driver's side door and grabbed the handle. "Fuck it. Let's go home."

We all climbed into the Love Boat for our trip home.

212

A hand slides an 8-track cassette into the car stereo.

Music blares from the speakers.

*"Why do we never get an answer
When we're knocking at the door?
Because the truth is hard to swallow
That's what the war of love is for"*

-The Moody Blues

****

We drove all night in utter silence, only stopping once so Beef could go to the bathroom, and even then, he just did his quick business and we got right back on the road.

Kevin drove. I was on the passenger side. Joe and Beef in the back. We all stared blankly out the windows so we wouldn't have to look at each other.

It certainly wasn't the same as our fun trip out.

And we certainly weren't the same people.

Once we got back to Boston, Joe and I checked into a hotel. We needed to suit up and get ready for Jimmy's funeral.

I ducked down to the sink in my room and rinsed my face with cold water, then stared deeply at my reflection in the mirror. I was struggling with the decisions I'd made.

But apparently, I wasn't the only one...

--Katie was getting dressed and ready at her father's house. She stared at her reflection in the mirror, then sadly removed her wedding ring and placed legal divorce papers into her purse.

--At the Eire Pub, the McShane brothers sat on their barstools. Corey dropped the cell phone from his ear and nodded to his brother.

"They're at the deli."

Ronan opened his coat and discretely slid a handgun down onto his brothers' lap.

--Joe stood inside his hotel room and slid on a pair of black Ray Ban sunglasses. Full of Rockstar bravado, he opened the window, attempted to lift the oversized TV from its stand, but tweaked his back and gave up.

--Beef stood in the family Deli and scanned photos on the wall, generations of the burly men who had owned the store before him. He looked down and snapped the silver buckles shut on the black guitar case that held Jimmy's prized Carlton Fisk baseball bat.

--Kevin sat behind the wheel of the Love Boat and looked to the passenger seat. It was the seat that used to belong to his girlfriend Katie. The seat that used to belong to his best friend Jimmy. Now the only thing sitting there was his beloved case of 8-track tapes.

--Detective Richie Kelly opened the cigar box filled with old photos of two Police Academy cadets. Richie Kelly and Bill Callahan. Both men in younger days. Better days. He lit his cigar and let a flume of smoke circle the room.

-- Officer Powers sat in a squad car across the street from Beef's Deli, waiting and watching as the long black hearse pulled down the alley.

I took a deep breath and hesitated over my cell phone for a minute or two, not really wanting to make this next call, but knowing I had to. Someone on the other end of the phone answered.

I took a deep breath and said, "Detective Kelly, please."

****

Jimmy's funeral was an hour away, so we had to move fast. Kevin opened the rear door of the hearse and shouted, "Wake up!"

The driver bolted upright and squinted at the morning sunlight as Joe stepped forward and flashed him an ID badge. It had been a rough 24 hours for this guy. He lost a body in his charge, spent the night sleeping in the back of a hearse, and now he had an IRS agent rousing him from a dead sleep. The poor guy should have stayed in Cleveland.

"Sir. My name is Joe Coughlan with the Internal Revenue Service," Joe said in his best 'I'm just another prying Government asshole' voice. "Could I ask you to climb out of the casket please?"

Kevin whispered, "Bet you never had to say that before."

"You'd be surprised," Joe whispered back, then turned his attention to the driver. "You work for DeVito Funeral home in Cleveland, Ohio. Is that correct, sir?"

"Yes," the bleary-eyed driver replied.

"And you've been employed there for how long?"

"Eight years."

Joe stayed in perfect central-casting Internal Revenue Service character. Grumpy, official, all business.

"Mmm, hmm. Tell me. Have you ever used this vehicle for purposes other than funeral transportation?"

The driver didn't answer.

"It's come to our attention, sir, that you've had outside income other than that of your primary employer," Joe said, then referred to a blank piece of paper to make it all seem official. "The, ahem, Fuzzy Buggy?'"

The driver turned ash white.

"I...I drive some of the girls places. Sometimes. In the limo. But just sometimes. Like, Mondays and Tuesdays. And weekends. And a few holidays. Well, maybe a lot."

Joe leaned forward and finally broke character.

"Dude, you can't write off 'Amish Fetish' as a business expense."

Kevin stepped in. "We have a bit of *'business'* to attend to ourselves. And we could use your help."

With that, the driver slowly began to climb out of the casket, his clothes a crumpled mess.

"Let's go!" Joe snapped. "Churn baby, churn!"

****

We all met up in the alley behind Beef's Deli, the Love Boat was parked beside the hearse.

"Explain to me again why you needed a carcass of meat?" Beef asked Kevin, a bit annoyed.

"Because we had to fill the casket with something, idiot," Kevin replied.

"You didn't take my Omaha steaks, did you? Use the pork. It's on Special this week," Beef pleaded.

"Only the best for Jimmy," Joe added.

I was starting to feel uncomfortable since I had a lot on my mind.

"Listen guys, I need to tell you something," I started to say, but I never got the chance to finish.

A car roared into the alley and the McShane brothers climbed out.

"Aw, is that me dead junkie brother in there?" Corey mocked.

Kevin took a step in their direction, but Beef put an arm on his shoulder to stop him.

"Mind yourself, boyo. Not unless you want to join your friend in the box there," Ronan sneered, then pulled a gun from his belt and handed it to Corey. "And here-in lies your example, brother. Finish it."

"Wait," Beef pleaded to Corey. "I told you I'd get the bat. You said your brother would…"

"Your brother would, what?" Ronan snarled. "Let youse go? What is this, 'Good Cop/Bad Cop?'"

Suddenly, the sharp squawk of a police siren sliced the morning air.

"And *that* would be a **real** Cop," Joe said as a cruiser pulled up the alley.

Ronan reached out and quickly grabbed the guitar case from Beef's hand.

Kevin glared at me with a face full of accusation.

"How do the cops know we're here?!"

We all stood motionless as white-haired Officer Powers climbed out of the cruiser.

Joe looked at his watch and grumbled, "I knew we'd never make it."

"Shut the fuck up!" we all shouted in unison.

Officer Powers surveyed the situation.

"Interesting way to mourn here, gentlemen."

He looked quizzically at the guitar case in Ronan's hand.

"Bagpipes," Ronan told him. "For our dear brother's funeral."

"Jesus, I hate those things," Powers replied, then motioned for them to leave. "It's not you I'm here for."

The McShanes hopped into their car and drove away. Powers turned to face us.

"So, what do you boys have against Swedish Rock bands?"

"We're innocent!" Beef exclaimed. "It was the security guard!"

"Good for him," Kevin said. "ABBA shouldn't even be in the fuckin' Hall of Fame in the first place."

Powers smirked.   "You must be Sullivan. Detective Kelly would like to see you after the service."

A chill went through Kevin.

Powers turned to me. "Mr. Crowley, could you come with me please?"

I could see Kevin's eyes narrow with confusion and suspicion as I followed Officer Powers to his squad car.

Down the street and around the corner from the alley, the McShanes stood over their car. Ronan tossed the black guitar case onto the hood, anxious to finally have the Carlton Fisk bat in his possession.

Silver buckles snapped open.

Ronan's eyes grew wide and his face twisted red with anger. There, laid upon the plush red velvet, was a plastic yellow wiffleball bat. Sand poured out from the hollow tip as Ronan held it in his hands.

He tossed it into the car and they headed for the church.

Back in the alley, Officer Powers pulled away in his cruiser, waving a copy of my book in his hand.

Kevin glared at me.

"The fuck was that all about?"

"Nothing," I deflected. "He just wanted an autograph."

"So, he's just gonna let us go?" Beef asked.

"How did he know we were here, Mike?" Kevin demanded.

They all stared, waiting. I felt cornered. I stammered a bit.

"I..I told you guys. I can't be involved in all this."

"I knew it," Kevin blurted. "He told the cops. That's why he was on the phone this whole trip. You'll never change."

I was done.

"You know what? Fuck you, Kevin. Look me up if you're ever in LA, boys."

I turned and walked away.

"Come on, Mike. Please," Beef pleaded.

"With or without you, we're gonna do this," Kevin called out. "Jimmy needs a proper funeral."

I'm not sure what it was that made me stop. Maybe it was guilt. Maybe it was hearing Jimmy's name. But when I turned around, I could see the determination in each of their faces.

I gave a resigned sigh.

"So. Where are we gonna bury him?"

"I didn't say we were gonna bury him," Kevin said with that same shit-eatin' grin he had when he convinced us all to drive to Cleveland.

"I said Jimmy needs a *proper* funeral...for the Norseman he is."

A hand slides an 8-track cassette into the car stereo.

Music plays on the speakers.

"The roses in the window box
Have tilted to one side
Everything about this house
Was born to grow and die"

-Elton John

ST. MARK CHURCH – Dorchester, MA

We stood on the back steps of the church and watched as the casket was removed from the hearse, holding our breath hoping the whole meat-instead-of-Jimmy switch was going to work.

Mourners, all locals who never miss a chance to attend a good mid-week funeral, began to file in. They were all well-behaved, all uncomfortable in suits and ties, talking quietly, shaking hands, each giving sad sympathetic smiles and pats on the shoulder.

Not us. The tension between the four of us was palpable, especially me and Kevin.

"They're gonna know something's up," I whispered to him out the corner of my mouth.

"We're fine," Kevin loudly Irish-whispered back.

"This is a stupid idea."

"Jesus, you are such a pussy."

Beef scolded us. "Shhh. Guys. We're in Church."

I leaned to Kevin. "Try not to make a move on Mrs. Callahan. I know how you like vulnerable women."

"Try not to steal any passages from the Bible for your next book."

"Grease monkey," I said.

"Hollywood douche," he snapped.

"Guys! You're gonna get us in trouble," Beef said even louder.

"Shut up," the two of us shot back.

Joe stood beside us tapping at his watch.

"I knew we'd make it," he said with a huge smile of confidence.

"Shut up!" the three of us shot back.

Katie was making her way up the old granite steps. She looked beautiful. Katie always looked beautiful. The last time we spoke was when she called to tell me about Jimmy, and that was a brief, sad conversation. We made slight eye contact, and she greeted all the guys with a warm, heartfelt embrace, kissing each of them gently on the cheek as she managed somehow to hold back her tears. She collected herself and turned to Beef.

"Stevie, Mrs. Callahan wants you to do a reading," Katie said removing a folded note from her purse.

"Me? What? There must be some kind of mistake. I'm sure she meant Mike," Beef nervously replied.

"Nope. Mrs. Callahan said *'that'* Steven," Katie told him with a knowing smirk.

Beef immediately began to panic. He looked at the reading, then showed the paper to Joe.

"What's this word?" he asked.

"Propitiation."

"Prop…prodiditate…propagate…"

He was a mess.

Beef struggled with easy words, but this was a Websters Dictionary nightmare. He began to scribble over the reading with a pen.

"I'm not saying it," he said. "This one too. Nope. Too many vowels."

"Oh great, now we're rewriting the Gospels," I groaned.

"I'm just gonna wing it," Beef said.

"Wise choice. I'm pretty sure that's how the Prophets did it," Joe remarked.

"It's not Open Mic Night, Beef. Just stick to the fuckin' script," Kevin told him.

"I think you mean Script*ure*," said Joe.

Beef was a nervous wreck. Then, he began to sweat.

"Oh boy...here it comes...you guys *know* I have a gland issue," he said in full panic mode as he reached into his pocket for the emergency Snickers bar.

"Shit. Here we go," Kevin said rolling his eyes.

"Maybe there's a mop in the rectory," Joe deadpanned.

Katie tenderly took the Snickers bar, wrapped it in Beef's handkerchief and said, "You'll be fine, Stevie. Save it for later."

She looked at all of us. "You guys heading down the Cape after the service?"

"You coming?" Beef asked enthusiastically.

"Naw, you guys finish your road trip'" she said then looked at Kevin with a smirk, "Chicks do get it."

****

As I sat in church that day waiting for my friend's service to begin, I started to realize that Kevin was right. I'm a pretty rotten, superficial person. And that truth terrified me. When I mentioned how Kate and I used to go to parties - this one's an asshole, this one's a prick, this one's a loser - I realized all those difficult people I hate are me.

They're all me.

The congregation sat up as an elderly Priest slowly approached the pulpit. The Reverend E. Joseph Burke. We couldn't believe he was still alive. I mean, Jesus, the guy must have been 100 twenty-five years ago when he taught us back in high school! All I could remember about Father Burke was that he dabbled in racism and could play a mean boogie-woogie piano. (There was one in the school cafeteria and 'Burkie' would play it for us every chance he got. That is when he wasn't berating the black students from Columbia Point.)

Father Burke looked out to the crowded church.

"Our first reading will be from one of James' early childhood friends. Beef...I mean Steven. Just, just Steven."

Beef nervously approached the altar, sweating profusely, almost translucent, his shirt a stained mess of perspiration. He took his place at the pulpit, removed the piece of paper from his breast pocket and looked down in horror. The reading was soaked. The words completely smudged and unintelligible.

Joe closed his eyes and began to mumble incoherently. Kevin leaned and whispered, "Are you praying?"

"Yeah," Joe replied out the corner of his mouth. "I'm praying his mic is grounded."

Beef looked down at the unintelligible wet paper in his hand and mumbled into the microphone, "I, um, I have a gland problem."

He was frazzled and looked out at the faces in the church waiting on his every word.

"Geeze, all this sweat," he said, clearly uncomfortable. "Okay," he started. "Um, a reading … a reading from the Book According to Bruce. And a few other guys."

Oh no.

He was gonna wing it.

Shit.

Beef cleared his throat and began to address the congregation.

"*In the day we **sweat** out on the streets of a runaway American dream.*"

Father Burke looked at the Bible on his lap and began to flip through the pages, not exactly sure where this reading was from.

Beef continued.

"You can dance, you can jive. Having the time of your life."

Kevin leaned to Joe and grumbled, "Sweet Jesus. Is that ABBA?!"

"Yep. I do believe it is," Joe nodded.

"God help us," I put my face in my hands.

Beef was now a complete train wreck sweaty mess. He reached for the hanky in his suit pocket to wipe his forehead, and unknowingly smeared chocolate from the emergency Snickers bar all over his face.

Aaaaand our good old goofy man-child Beef was back.

Completely covered in chocolate and dripping with sweat, Beef looked to us for support. We unanimously shot him enthusiastic 'thumbs up' signs and pantomimed support.

We are such assholes.

He continued.

"I can't get no satisfaction," Beef declared. *"He can't get no satisfaction. 'Cause I try, and he tries, and we try, try, try."*

The congregation looked at each other and shifted in their seats, confused. Mrs. Callahan sat clutching on a Kleenex with Katie beside her, an arm wrapped close. She sobbed loudly, "Oh, my Jimmy!"

Beef clearly needed help.

We could all see that.

Suddenly, Joe shot up from the pew. He pumped his arms above his head, and screamed, "Rock and Roll!"

Beef smiled at the gesture.

He wiped the chocolate off his face, cleared his throat, and said, "Okay. I got this."

Then Beef sort of looked to the sky for inspiration. To God? To Jimmy? To Milton Hershey? I have no idea, but suddenly his face was filled with a newfound confidence.

He began to recite.

"As I walk through this wicked world searching for light in the darkness of insanity. I ask myself; Is all hope lost?"

The congregation began to nod quietly, and Beef built even more confidence.

"Is there only pain and hatred and misery?"

He grabbed the microphone, his voice now booming, every word reverberating with powerful energy like a Southern Baptist Preacher.

"And each time I feel like this inside, there's one thing... I said there's <u>ONE</u> thing I want to know!"

The crowd was getting into it, heads bobbing, people hanging on his every word.

"What's so funny about peace, love and understanding?"

The congregation responded.

"Amen brother." "Praise Jesus."

"Amen indeed," Beef replied, full of bravado and Baptist swag.

He paused, closed his eyes reverently, and said, *"'And she's buying... a stairway...to...heaven.'* Ah - men."

And then, with a dramatic mic-drop, Beef stepped down from the pulpit, and re-joined us in the front pew.

Mrs. Callahan leaned to Katie and whispered, "I always liked that Steven."

****

We walked out into the funeral's daylight as family began to crowd around Mrs. Callahan and offer their condolences. A few people stopped to congratulate Beef on his inspirational speech, and he loved the attention, shaking each hand with a "Thank you, sister." "Go with God, brother." "My voice is merely a vessel."

Father Burke approached with a stern yet heavenly look on his face.

"Quite an interesting eulogy there, Steven."

Beef was speechless.

"Well, God Bless you, boys," Father Burke said, then leaned towards Beef and whispered, "And God Bless Elvis Costello."

Detective Kelly was making his way down the aisle. He shook each of our hands with a cocky air of confidence.

"So glad you could all make it," he said, then taking us all in with his gaze, asked, "and where is Mr. Sullivan?"

"He's outside, getting the car," Beef told him.

"Of course. The infamous Love Boat," Kelly replied.

"You still driving that Crown Vic? Nice radio as I recall," Joe winked.

Kelly wasn't in a mood for jokes.

"I'll see you boys at the cemetery," he said before looking directly at Beef with a knowing eye. "We need to discuss some 'Red Sox history.'"

Beef squirmed.

Shit.

Kelly knew about the bat.

****

Kevin was standing alone by the hearse when the McShane brothers approached him from behind.

"Shame about your garage," Ronan sneered.

"The fuck are you talkin' about?!" Kevin snapped as he spun around.

"The Deli man's car. It may get a bit 'overheated' when it starts," Ronan replied with a glint of madness in his eye.

Kevin's jaw tightened.

He glared at the psycho Irishman.

"Anything happens to my son, I'll fuckin' kill you both."

"So, where's the bat?" Ronan asked, not in the mood for any of Kevin's heroics.

"Last time I saw it, it was swingin' against your old man's skull," Kevin replied with equal venom.

They stood eye to eye, like two gunfighters preparing for battle. Ronan leaned in close to Kevin's ear and snarled, "Stupid, Yank. Did you really think I'd let you get away with this?"

Always the toughest guy in any fight, Kevin leaned in and snarled right back.

"Did you really think I'd let your prick father?"

Maybe it was just his eyes, but Kevin could see that rattled him.

****

On the other side of Dorchester, Billy sat in the driver's seat fiddling with a set of car keys. When he found the correct one, he inserted it into the steering column and turned the ignition from LOCK to ON, unaware of the danger around him.

He stepped on the gas pedal.

The car wouldn't turn over.

He tried again.

Nothing.

He pumped the gas one more time.

Nothing.

The engine fired, then missed.

Finally, Billy pounded his fist on the steering wheel and screamed, "COME ON!"

The idiot lights on the dashboard flickered.

Billy was behind the wheel of the Bonneville, not Beef's minivan.

Exhaust blew past the DISCO SUCKS bumper sticker and the powerful engine of the Love Boat roared to life. He stomped on the accelerator pedal and a scream of rubber kissed off the concrete as the Love Boat peeled out from the alley behind Beef's deli.

Billy slid an 8-track cassette into the stereo and cranked the volume to 11. The enormous car filled with the sound of Earth, Wind and Fire's 'September' blaring from the Pioneer speakers.

> *'Ba de ya, say do you remember*
> *Ba de ya, dancing in September*
> *Ba de ya, never was a cloudy day'*

This was the first time Billy had ever driven the Love Boat.

And he was loving it!

He looked small behind the wheel as he sped furiously through the streets, his heart beating fast, his face beaming.

'Hey hey hey
Ba de ya, say do you remember
Ba de ya, dancing in September
Ba de ya, never was a cloudy day'

Suddenly, the music stopped.

The stereo began to spew magnetic 8-track tape.

"Shitshitshitshitshit!" Billy shouted, simultaneously trying to maneuver the car and stop the 'bleeding' 8-track tape player.

He looked up at the last minute.

"SHIIIIIIT!"

There was a *SCREECH* of tires as the Love Boat stopped inches from the long black hearse.

Kevin and the McShanes jumped.

Suddenly, Beef came from out of nowhere and with a mighty swing of the wiffleball bat, he screamed, "I'm not fat!"

Sand whipped from the hollow plastic tip, blinding Corey and Ronan.

Ronan swung at Kevin, his red eyes bulging with fury when-- *CRACK!* a punch caught him square on the jaw.

All the commotion caused the crowd to start making their way towards us, so the McShane boys took that as their cue to run. They scampered away like cockroaches in the light.

Kevin turned to me.

"Thanks, man."

"No problem," I nodded, then gave a wink, "Gimme 5!"

We slapped five and I winced in pain, pretty sure that I broke my hand on Ronan's jaw.

Kevin walked over and poked his head in the driver's side window of the Love Boat. Billy was sitting there, shell-shocked, his lap completely covered in 8-track tape.

"I...I couldn't stop it," was all he could say. "It just kept coming and coming. It was awful, dude. Awful!"

"You really saved my ass there, Bill," Kevin said.

He opened the car door and a mound of twisted 8-track tape fell to the ground.

"Guess those old tapes are good for something," Billy replied.

Kevin smiled at his son.

"Listen, don't go anywhere near the garage. I think those McShane's did something to Beef's car. I'll check it out when I get back."

"Where are you going now?" Billy asked, his face full of disappointment.

"I got one more ride I gotta take with Jimmy and the guys," Kevin said, then looked his son in the eye. "But I was thinking, when I get back, maybe you and I can take our own road trip. Okay...*bro*?"

"Okay...*Dad*," Billy replied.

His face was beaming.

So was Kevin's.

****

I didn't see Katie coming up behind me. I just heard her voice whisper softly, "My God. The Love Boat."

Her eyes were puffy from crying and I wasn't sure if it was from the service or just the finality of everything.

We both stood there staring at the Bonneville.

"We had some great times in that car," I said searching her eyes. The ground. The sky. Then her eyes again.

"We did," Katie replied softly.

She turned to face me. "When you didn't show up at the lawyer's office, I thought..."

She didn't finish the sentence. Her words just hung in the air between us until I finally found the courage to look at her eyes.

"Katie..."

But I stopped.

What I wanted to say, what I *should* have said was, 'I'm sorry. I'm so sorry. I'm a selfish asshole. I've loved you since we were kids, and I'm so sorry I've been such a jerk.' Then I should have grabbed her around the waist and kissed her long and hard.

But I didn't.

The back of my throat tightened, and I got a knot in my stomach. No words came out of my mouth. Me. The guy who talked his way past Lenny Palmer the Meatloaf-looking Security Guard at The Rock and Roll Hall of Fame. The smarmy, cheesy Hollywood salesman of late-night infomercials. I was speechless. A pimple-faced teenage loser again.

Katie reached into her purse and handed me the envelope containing our divorce papers.

"They just need your signature," she said.

As Katie turned the corner out of view, I didn't see her lean her back to the building and sink to the floor, crumpling into silent tears.

And she didn't see me wipe my moist eyes with the back of my hand.

The guys quietly came to my side.

"Let's finish this," I told them.

Then the four of us climbed into the Love Boat for one last road trip.

A hand slides an 8-track cassette into the car stereo.

Music plays on the speakers.

*"Well, I dreamed I saw the knights in armor coming,
Saying something about a queen.
There were peasants singing and drummers drumming
And the archer split the tree.*

*Look at Mother Nature on the run
In the nineteen seventies."*

-Neil Young

****

The four of us stared out the window in silence as the Love Boat drove south to the flexed arm of Cape Cod.

What we didn't know was that the McShane brothers were following us a few cars back.

What we *also* didn't know once we made it to the beach, *our* beach on Lewis Bay, was that two separate and distinctly different services were occurring simultaneously.

As the Love Boat drove along a sandy beach road, the hearse drove along a flowing green cemetery.

As we carried the body bag out of the Love Boat's trunk, the casket was slid from the back of the hearse.

As we lowered the thick plastic body bag into the old Dory rowboat, the mahogany casket was lowered into a deep grave.

We placed branches and wood over the boat.

Mourners placed flowers and greens over the casket.

The four of us stood solemnly on the beach, while mourners stood solemnly by the grave site.

Father Burke began to speak to the assembled crowd.

"Our friend James has come to you now. As he kneels before you, know how much he was loved in this life, and how many he loved in return. Watch over him as he crosses the bridge from this life to the next. And welcome him with glory, that he may live on forever in our hearts."

Katie leaned in and said, "That was beautiful, Father. Old Testament?"

"Viking Prayer for the Dead," Father Burke replied with a smirk. "Figured Jimmy would have liked that."

Detective Kelly looked around at the mourners gathered by the grave, his eyes scanning the crowd.

No McShane brothers.

No guys.

Something was up.

He repeated one of Father Burke's verses aloud.

"*Watch over him as he crosses the bridge.*"

A light bulb went off.

Kelly hopped into his Crown Vic and headed south towards the Sagamore Bridge.

LEWIS BAY – WEST YARMOUTH, MA

Kevin looked up and down the beach, taking it all in. The sun was about to set as the flat gentle surf swished against the sand. He stared out at Lewis Bay for a moment, then turned to the group.

"Alright, fellow Norsemen. You guys bring your 'Offerings'?"

Beef went first.

He walked to the Dory rowboat with the half-finished Viking ship model he took from Jimmy's apartment.

"Thought Jimmy might want to finish this," he said then softly laid the plastic ship among the branches and wood.

Joe was next.

He walked to the tiny boat, reached into his coat pocket, and removed a pair of thick black-rimmed eyeglasses.

"Here you go Jimmy. It's a little something I picked up from the Rock and Roll Hall of Fame."

We all looked at each other.

"Wait. You stole Elvis Costello's glasses?" I asked.

"Don't be crazy," Joe said, placing them into the boat alongside the model Viking ship. "They're Buddy Holly's."

It was my turn.

I walked up to the boat.

After a moment of thought, I removed an envelope from my blazer, ripped it in half and placed the divorce papers alongside Joe's glasses and Beef's plastic model. Then, figuring Jimmy might want some of our beach wherever he was, I bent down for a handful of sand and slowly let it pour from my fingers and into the rowboat.

Satisfied, I joined Beef and Joe.

And then we waited.

Kevin was the last to go.

He stood for a long time staring down at the boat, at his friend, silently saying goodbye, and sorry. I know in his soul Kevin felt he had something to do with Jimmy's death, but that couldn't be further from the truth.

Kevin looked back at me and smiled a little bit, then he bent down and let his hand scan a row of classic rock 8-track tapes. Rolling Stones. Led Zeppelin. The Who.

Wait. It should be The Who, *then* Zeppelin.

He arranged them in proper alphabetical order one last time, then Kevin placed his beloved case of 8-track tapes carefully, reverently, alongside the other offerings.

We smiled.

It all felt right.

"Wait. I almost forgot," Beef said then ran back to the Love Boat. He dug under the seat and, to our surprise, he returned with the Carlton Fisk bat.

Oh. My. God.

Our husky, sweaty, loveable man-child friend pulled a fast one on those redheaded prick McShane brothers!

Well, almost.

Just as he was about to place the bat into the rowboat, we heard, "Hold it right there."

The McShane brothers were behind us.

Psycho Ronan grabbed the bat from Beef's hand.

"Batter up," he snarled, his yellow teeth flashed as he cocked the bat back. "That what you Yanks say?"

Beef squinted, preparing for the blow when suddenly a voice boomed from across the beach.

"Do it and you can kiss your fuckin' Blarney Stones goodbye."

For the second time in a week, a gun was pointed in our direction.

This time, it was Detective Richie Kelly.

It had been years since Richie Kelly unholstered his gun, let alone aim it, but he had a good cop stance, and you could tell it felt good to him, especially since that aim was pointed directly at Ronan's groin.

"Easy, now," Ronan implored. "What are you comin' at us for? Your man, the mechanic there. He killed me Da!"

Now, even though I had a gun pointed in my direction, like, *a lot,* this week, I think I could tell the difference between someone who exposes a gun for show, like the McShanes, and someone who actually knows how to use it. Richie Kelly was clearly a man who knew how to use it. He levelled the gun from Ronan's 'Blarney Stones' to Ronan's head, then curled his finger around the trigger.

The McShane's knew he meant business.

"I could give three shits about your *Da*. We looked everywhere. Never did find a murder weapon," Kelly said, dripping with sarcasm.

He took the Carlton Fisk bat from Ronan's hand. "Now, go. This is a private party."

The McShanes scurried away, stumbling over the dunes and hurrying down a sand path until they came face to face with Officer Powers, who stood dangling a small bag of heroin, all neatly wrapped in a printed cocktail napkin from the Eire Pub.

The redheaded pricks were finally busted.

Powers immediately cuffed them both.

Back at the beach, Kelly turned his attention to us and the rowboat. "You boys really thought you could pull this off, huh?"

"The McShanes. They were gonna..." Beef started, but Kelly held up a hand.

"I wouldn't worry about the McShanes. We got enough to put them away in a nice big red, white and blue, Yankee Doodle, American prison. What did you call it on the phone, Mr. Crowley? 'Finance and Pharmaceuticals?'"

The guys all looked at me in shock.

I just shrugged. After all, Point Two of my '5 Point Plan for Success' is **Loyalty.**

Detective Kelly turned to Kevin.

"Now, Mr. Sullivan. I believe we have some unfinished business."

Kevin's shoulders dropped. This was the end. He'd been carrying the weight and the guilt for too long, and this was his punishment.

He closed his eyes, held his arms out and awaited his handcuffs. But when he looked up, instead of handcuffs in his outstretched hands, Kelly laid the Carlton Fisk bat.

Kevin was stunned.

We all were.

"Go on," Kelly said motioning him toward the boat. "Put it where it belongs."

Kevin was at first confused, but then he understood. He placed the bat in alongside the other offerings.

Richie Kelly walked to the side of the boat and scanned the scene, rubbing the back of his neck and looking deeply at body bag that held Bill Callahan's son.

"I made a casket-side promise to protect Bill's wife and kid. I shoulda done more," he said, then pulled the Coroner's report from his coat pocket. "Only five months till my thirty. Fuck it. Let the next guy try and explain all of this."

Kelly looked back at us. Four middle-aged men standing on a beach at dusk, still in dark suits from their friend's funeral. And in that moment, Richie Kelly had the answer to his question. People *do* still have friendships like the one he shared with Bill Callahan.

He placed the Coroner's report into the old Dory rowboat, lit a cigar, and tossed the matches to Kevin.

"It's good to keep a promise to an old friend," he said with a smirk.

Then Richie Kelly climbed into his Crown Vic, set the radio to one of the pre-set easy-listening stations, and pulled away.

****

Sticks were ignited and the flames rose.

We stood on the shoreline and silently watched as the rowboat drifted further and further into the bay, the flames reflecting off the water and in the faces of four life-long grown friends. The only sound was the crackling of the burning wood and the soft break of the ocean water slushing onto the shoreline.

We took off our shoes and pushed our feet into the cool, soft sand. I felt something buried beneath my foot. I reached down and found an old, rusted bottle cap. I smiled at the symbolism. It was as if Jimmy left it there to preserve a ritual. And for a moment part of me wondered if he somehow orchestrated this whole crazy adventure.

I snapped the cap at Beef.

He ducked, and we all smiled. And in that moment, it seemed like none of us had grown up.

We were eighteen again.

Teenagers.

The best of friends.

"God, I miss this place," Joe said.

"You guys really think that was Carleton Fisk's bat?" Beef asked.

"Naw. It was just..." Kevin began, but I finished the sentence for him.

"It was just something to hold onto."

We looked at each other and shared a smile.

"I'll make sure you don't lose that deli, Beef," I said, rubbing my right hand still swollen from landing on Ronan's iron jaw. "Where else could Katie and I get a good sandwich back home?"

"Maybe you should show the bank your 'The 10-inch Beef special,'" Joe said. "It sure was a big hit in Amish country."

Beef playfully punched Joe on the arm.

"So, the glasses from the Rock and Roll Hall of Fame. They're fake too?" he asked.

"Nope. They're Buddy Holly's alright," Joe replied with that ironic smile of his. "I would have grabbed a guitar too if the alarms didn't go off."

"Stealing Joe?" Kevin said, dripping with sarcasm. "Now how is that gonna look on your White House job application?"

"I'm done with the whole lawyer thing," Joe replied.

And I think it was the first time I ever saw Joe happy.

Like, really happy.

"Think I'm gonna buy a bar," he said staring out to the bay. "Maybe start a '70s cover band. 'EZ Joe and the Loopholes.'"

Kevin nodded his approval and said simply, "Rock n' Roll."

Beef spoke up.

"Guys, I don't mean to be weird or anything but, something smells really good."

"It should," Kevin replied, pointing to the rowboat engulfed in flames on the flat water. "That's top choice, Grade A sirloin out there."

We all looked at Kevin.

"I had the driver make the switch. What do you think this is, 400 A.D? I'm not gonna torch Jimmy. Besides, it's against the law."

I couldn't help but laugh.

"*Now* you care about breaking the law?"

"So, where's Jimmy?" Joe asked.

Before Kevin could answer, I spoke up. "Actually, Jimmy is where he belongs. With his dad in Braintree, overlooking the highway to Cape Cod."

They all look at me, incredulous.

Especially Kevin.

I held up my ever-present cell phone.

"You guys were right. I did make a lot of calls on this trip. One was to Detective Kelly letting him know about the heroin and the McShanes. One to Mrs. Callahan letting her know I changed cemetery locations. And one was to the Funeral Home to take care of the burial. I mean, we couldn't expect Kevin to think of everything on this road trip, could we?"

I leaned and whispered to Kevin. "By the way, you can stop sending that envelope to Mrs. Callahan. She thinks it's been me this whole time."

Kevin was a bit dumbfounded, but quickly realized that I found out. He looked at me and gave me a quiet nod.

The nod.

The one I wanted and envied and craved so much as a teenager.

Then Kevin did something strange and wonderful. It's hard to describe, but he kind of looked through me to the ocean, like he was looking to the past, remembering all the best times of his life. That Thanksgiving football game. The day his son was born. Our high school graduation.

And today.

This very moment.

Everything was perfectly clear to him, and perfectly right.

"But I thought Jimmy wanted a Viking Funeral," Beef said.

"It was never about the funeral, Beef," Kevin said. "The Love Boat. The Cape. This. *This* is what Jimmy wanted. All of us together. Always."

Kevin looked out at Lewis Bay toward the burning boat as it melted into a glorious red sunset, the color of the flames and the color of the sky melting into one.

He breathed the salt air deep into his lungs.

"He's at peace. The ocean heals everything."

We all smiled and clutched that knowledge to our hearts.

Beef raised a beer.

"To Jimmy."

We joined him and smiled goodbye to our friend.

"To us," I said. "The Norsemen."

A hand slides an 8-track cassette into the car stereo. Music plays from the car speakers.

*"I don't know what happens when people die
Can't seem to grasp it as hard as I try
It's like a song playing right in my ear
That I can't sing
I can't help listening"*

-Jackson Browne

When I think back on that year, our Senior year of high school, it seems like I could measure it out in blocks of music, like Kevin's rows of cassettes. There was Rock in the summer as we prepared for football season listening to The Rolling Stones, Blue Oyster Cult, Tom Petty and the Heartbreakers. There were dance tunes in the winter at house parties with Barry White, and Earth Wind & Fire. And there was the Indie Punk Springtime when we all thought we were cool listening to Devo, English Beat and The Sex Pistols.

I knew when I decided to write this story it was crazy. I mean, who the hell would believe a bunch of grown men would drive their dead friend hundreds of miles home?

But we did.

Believe it or not, we did.

And I'd like to think Jimmy loved every minute of it.

I've written self-help books, so this is just another one, right? It's a story about friendship, and I don't care if anyone buys it or even reads it. It's mine, like that sunrise in Cleveland. This story belongs to us. Me and Joe and Beef and Kevin… and Jimmy.

My best friends.

Everyone needs people like them in your life. People you can just be yourself with, say shit and act like an asshole, and bust balls, and it doesn't matter. It doesn't matter if you're a Washington lawyer, or a car mechanic, or you own a Delicatessen or you're a phony big-shot Hollywood celebrity. We know each other, maybe better now than when we were young. Kevin is the angry one. Jimmy the lost one. Beef the child. Joe the clown. And me? Well, I guess I'm the idiot.

They say the best time machine is a song. There's something special and magical about music, how it evokes a memory and causes emotions to rush over you. There are people with Alzheimer's and Dementia, people who can't even recognize their wives or husbands or children, but suddenly a song comes on and their face lights up, and they know every word to 'Hey Jude' by the Beatles or 'Beyond the

Sea' by Bobby Darin. It's subconscious and sublime and as deep as the ocean.

It's like that with old friends.

When you're together, there's a feeling of joy and comfort that you just don't have with other people. Time and experience take you away, but when you get back together, thick memories brush by like they just happened yesterday. You remember little details, like what you were wearing, how hard you laughed, and the song that was playing.

The music.

It's always the music.

Kevin was right. Music lasts forever.

And you have this total, absolute feeling of happiness. And love. Real love. The kind you know deep in your soul.

That's the way I feel about Katie.

My hand slid the 8-track cassette into the car stereo. (Yeah, it's been me playing the music this entire road trip.)

Hall and Oates blared from the speakers.

> *"Oh yeah, well well you*
> *You make my dreams come true*
> *Well well you, oh yeah*
> *You make my dreams come true"*

I turned the Cape Cod key chain dangling from the car ignition. Smoke blew past a faded DISCO SUCKS bumper sticker, and I pointed the Love Boat west for California.

MALIBU, CALIFORNIA

It was almost sunrise by the time I got to our house. At least it used to be our house. Katie is an early riser, so I knew she'd be up getting her morning coffee. She stiffened with surprise at the sight of me standing there at her front door, but she quickly gathered herself.

"Here to pick up your stuff?" Katie asked coldly.

"I can't go through with this, Kate," I said feeling lost and alone like never before in my entire life.

"Really? Well I'm confused, Mike. You want a divorce. You don't want a divorce. Come back when you know what you want," she said trying to close the door.

I stuck my hand out and stopped her.

"I'm sorry, Kate. I forgot about you. I forgot about a lot of things. But I know what I want. I want my best friend."

She could see that I was sincere.

To be fair, I'm not the same man, at least I hope I'm not.

I looked into her eyes.

"I thought running to the past and going on that road trip with my friends might help take my mind off things. In fact, it very much put my mind *on* things. I learned a lot about myself and I know what I want. I want to be a different person. A *better* person. A better friend. A better husband."

After a moment, she looked directly at me.

"Nothing happened, Mike. We're from Dorchester, not the Valley. We don't *'sleep with the pool boy'*," she said spitting the words and making them sound as ridiculous as she could.

I just stood there in awe. In awe of her beauty. Her ferocity. The way she's always right, or at least she's right enough to shut me up.

"This whole thing was all about your ego," she continued. "Nothing else mattered to you but your celebrity. You let your whole life fall away. You let me fall away."

Katie knows me better than anyone. She knows I can be a self-absorbed, brooding narcissist. My ego and insecurities got in the way and I felt sorry for myself since my book wasn't selling, so I made up some imaginary affair to deflect the hurt.

The thing is, there's something about Katie that makes you think you're not good enough, and a part of me was always trying to make her jealous. But jealousy was never part of her makeup. Katie is that confident. More confident than any of us guys, that's for sure.

She is Dorchester tough. A city girl to the core.

And in that moment, I realized something. When we were growing up everyone *wanted* Katie.

But not me.

I *needed* her.

"You know I'm just an insecure, selfish asshole," I said to her with a smirk.

Katie softened and gave me a small secret smile, the one that made the corner of her mouth curl. The one that every teenage boy in Dorchester fell in love with.

The one that I love.

"Better not let the Paparazzi hear you say that," she said with a smirk, then added, "I never asked for all of this, Mike. The house. The cars. It was never about that. I fell in love with you because you had dreams and drive and passion. I want *that*. I just want the guy I grew up with."

I thought to myself, 'When did I lose all that?' When did *we* lose that? Katie and I grew apart. Nothing worked consistently anymore. For a long time, our marriage worked like an old reliable car and we just didn't have the energy or desire to go shopping for a new one. I let us fall into something worse than extramarital affairs.

We fell into boring, comfortable routines of sameness.

We both stood there in the doorway looking at each other, not knowing the next move. I needed to do something. I needed to take responsibility for this current predicament, so I just went for it. I grabbed her around the waist and kissed her long and hard. It was the kind of kiss that we both took for granted. Deep and long and dizzying. So passionate that the ground gave way.

We were suddenly eighteen again.

In love and weak at the knees.

Katie pulled back and had to gather herself for a moment. She smiled, and her eyes spotted the car parked at the curb standing out among the palm trees and manicured lawns.

"Kevin sold you his Bonneville?" she asked, totally puzzled.

"It was a trade. I owed him. I owed them all," I said, then took her by the hand.

"We still have time. We could catch the sunrise together. A new day. A new beginning."

Katie squeezed my hand and smiled.

"I'd like that," she said. "I'd like that a lot."

EPILOGUE

XX Later that year I came back to Boston for another funeral. Beef's dad. Only this time we didn't stick the body in the trunk or try to burn it at a Viking Funeral.

We all showed up, The Four Norsemen, and went out for beers at The Banshee after the service to reminisce and laugh and tell stories and bust balls.

Just like old times.

Beef didn't have to pay off his loan to the McShanes. Those boys had quite a bit of illegal income from their 'Finance and Pharmaceuticals' business.

"You don't wash money like clothes," Joe told us. "You just juggle it around until someone like me comes crashing down on your head."

And Joe did. Hard.

He was able to pin a tax conviction on those Irish pricks. Corey and Ronan are doing time in a nice red, white and blue, Yankee Doodle prison.

That was the last audit Joe ever did.

He opened a bar in Pennsylvania. Amish country to be exact. Although he didn't start a rock band, the bar does have '70's cover bands perform every Thursday night.

We all wondered when he planned on bringing his new girlfriend to the Boston College Club. I would love to see the look on his old man's face when he met Hester, the Amish Milk Maid.

Speaking of girlfriends, Kevin met someone. He was at a record store in Dedham. (Where else, right?) Linda Walsh. She's lovely. Apparently, she liked his shiny red Porsche convertible (a trade is a trade) and Kevin liked her Rolling Stone concert t-shirt. Turns out, she bought the shirt at a Boston Garden concert in 1975. In a weird twist of fate, that was the first concert that both of them ever attended.

Pretty cool, right? Talk about timing.

Linda and Kevin are perfect for each other. Both are really passionate about music. Not obsessed...*passionate*.

And I realized something. I shouldn't knock people with passion, they turn out to be the most interesting people ever.

Last August Kevin and his son took a road trip to the Cape just before Billy started school. Kevin figured he'd spent the last 20 years trying to fix Jimmy and his problems, now it was time to work on his own.

Anyway, Kevin was in the passenger seat, fumbling with the iPod plugged into the stereo when Billy said, "Whoa, whoa, whoa. What are you doing?"

"Trying to play some music," Kevin snapped at him in typical Kevin style.

"Playing *some* music?" Billy replied. "What does that even mean? You set the mood for the entire road trip. Don't take this so lightly. Now, the first song in your Playlist is key. You need to make sure it's a good one."

Kevin just shook his head and grinned – apple not falling far from the tree and all that. He pointed to the armored knight logo printed on Billy's Holy Cross sweatshirt.

"That a Viking?" he asked.

"Crusader," Billy told him.

"Classic," Kevin said, smiling at the irony.

He handed Billy the iPod.

"Here, you pick the song."

Billy jumped in shock.

"Really?! Okay. This one is kind of an oldie," he said.

'Walk this Way' by Aerosmith and Run DMC blared from the speakers. If you really think about it, it was perfect. Classic Rock meets Hip Hop. At first, Kevin gave Billy a 'What the fuck is this?!' look.

He softened. Then actually smiled. He liked it!

Funny how things turn out sometimes, isn't it?

I can picture it all in my mind...

A Cape Cod key chain dangles from the car ignition.

A hand turns the key.

Exhaust blows past a DISCO **STILL** SUCKS bumper sticker.

The music blares as father and son cross the Sagamore Bridge.

269

Kevin smiles wide, his eyes closed as he feels the warm salt air on his face.

Just like Jimmy.

Don't you wish you could just freeze moments like this in your life, like old Polaroid pictures, stay in them and relive those moments in time again and again, and you could just float in the smells and the sounds and the feelings until you were ready to come out?

I sure do.

MIKE'S 8-TRACK ROAD TRIP PLAYLIST

What's So Funny About Peace Love and Understanding? - Elvis Costello

The Pretender - Jackson Brown

Dream On - Aerosmith

Roadhouse Blues - The Doors

Rock and Roll - Led Zeppelin

Taking Care of Business - Bachman Turner Overdrive

Let the Good Times Roll - The Cars

Paradise by the Dashboard Light - Meat Loaf

Hello Old Friend - Eric Clapton

Baba O'Riley - The Who

Needle and the Damage Done - Neil Young

Can't Get it Out of My Head - ELO

It's Over - Boz Scaggs

Turn the Page - Bob Seger

S.O.S. - ABBA

The Question – Moody Blues

Funeral for a Friend - Elton John

After the Gold Rush - Neil Young

For a Dancer - Jackson Brown

ABOUT THE AUTHOR

Mike is the founder of ChathamPoint Group, an executive search firm outside Boston. His 'midlife crisis' writing career began when his children and his money went off to college - checks made out to Loyola University Maryland (x2) and Assumption College respectively. Mike's work has placed in the NICHOLL FELLOWSHIP, BLUECAT, FINAL DRAFT Big Break and PAGE International screenplay competitions. Three of his screenplays were optioned and under development with production companies.

Mike is a graduate of Providence College and Boston College High School. He resides in Medfield, MA with his wife Michele. He spends summers on the beaches of Cape Cod and winters roaming the aisles of Home Depot.

contact: meb123@comcast.net

A FISHERMAN'S VIEW

After their mother's death, colorful Irish patriarch Michaleen Fitzgerald gives his estranged children three plastic baggies – RED, GREEN, YELLOW - to scatter her ashes at specific locations. The symbolism is not lost on them. Theresa is the angry one, Richard is materialistic, and Fiona is crippled with anxieties. But they're wrong. The colors represent something else entirely, and the journey to dispose the ashes and find their true meanings and destinations has just begun.

With dark but tender humor, Michaleen helps his children take a different view of life, hoping they'll grab it by the lapels and swing it back onto the dance floor, but each child is harboring complicated feelings and secrets that threaten to tear their family apart.

A FISHERMAN'S VIEW is a deeply emotional story of reconciliation and a celebration of family; how people who were raised so close can be so far apart without truly knowing it.

Available on Amazon.com

CROSSING GUARDS

Megan Hayes is a hospice nurse from the blue-collar streets of South Boston. Haunted by the memory of her mother dying in an empty house, Megan vows to never let a patient die alone. But with her Irish temper and bad dating record, Megan fears that she may never find love, and will ultimately end up alone herself.

    Living with her father doesn't help. Jackie Boy Hayes is a 68 year old, fitness-crazed former US Marine. Check that - no such thing as a former Marine. He IS a Marine! Jackie Boy spends his days seeking new and interesting ways to exercise, and finds an unlikely new recruit in a lonesome, overweight teenager. When Megan falls for a patient's married son, she will uncover shocking revelations and learn that there is more to life than waiting for it to end.

    CROSSING GUARDS is an uplifting story about finding love and friendship in unlikely places, reminding us to keep our hearts open and soldier on. Semper Fi

Available on Amazon.com

Made in the USA
Columbia, SC
24 May 2021